Harlequin
a brand-new

LUCY

The Cou

D0374053

These proud Italian aristrocrats are about to propose!

The Calvani family is a prosperous, aristocratic
Italian family headed by Count Francesco Calvani.

He has three nephews:

Guido—charming, easygoing and wealthy
in his own right, Guido is based in Venice.
He's heir to the Calvani title, but he doesn't want it....

Marco—aristocratic, sophisticated and very good-
looking, Marco is every woman's dream, managing
the family's banking and investments in Rome....

Leo—proud, rugged and athletic,
Leo is a reluctant tycoon, running the family's
prosperous farms in Tuscany.

The pressure is mounting on all three Calvani brothers
to marry and produce the next heirs
in the Calvani dynasty. Each will find a wife—
but will it be out of love or duty...?

Find out in this emotional,
exciting and dramatic trilogy:

April 2003—*The Venetian Playboy's Bride* #3744
June 2003—*The Italian Millionaire's Marriage* #3751
August 2003—*The Tuscan Tycoon's Wife* #3760

Don't miss it!

Dear Reader,

I always love the chance to write about Venice, because that city has been my second home since I married a Venetian. Perhaps that's why I think Venetians are the most romantic of men (although all other Italians come a close second). They combine emotional intensity with lightheartedness in a way that makes them irresistible.

Guido Calvani, the hero of *The Venetian Playboy's Bride*, is like that. He approaches life with a laugh and a conviction that he can make things happen the way he wants. But then, he's never met anyone like Dulcie, a private detective who's one step ahead, and it's only when it's too late that he discovers she's tied him in knots.

Their story is played out against Venice with its dark corners and mysterious alleys. In the city on the water nothing is ever quite what it seems, including Guido and Dulcie, who start by hiding their true selves, then learn, through love, to cast their masks aside.

After Guido comes Marco from Rome, cool and self-sufficient. Then Leo, the countryman from Tuscany. And always in the background is their uncle Francesco, Count Calvani, whose colorful life hides a romantic secret that takes them all by surprise.

Lucy Gordon

THE VENETIAN PLAYBOY'S BRIDE

Lucy Gordon

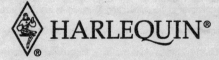

TORONTO • NEW YORK • LONDON
AMSTERDAM • PARIS • SYDNEY • HAMBURG
STOCKHOLM • ATHENS • TOKYO • MILAN • MADRID
PRAGUE • WARSAW • BUDAPEST • AUCKLAND

ISBN 0-373-03744-9

THE VENETIAN PLAYBOY'S BRIDE

First North American Publication 2003.

Copyright © 2003 by Lucy Gordon.

This edition published by arrangement with Harlequin Books S.A.

® and TM are trademarks of the publisher. Trademarks indicated with ® are registered in the United States Patent and Trademark Office, the Canadian Trade Marks Office and in other countries.

Visit us at www.eHarlequin.com

Printed in U.S.A.

CHAPTER ONE

GUIDO CALVANI took another turn along the hospital corridor, trying not to think of his uncle, lying behind the closed door, desperately ill.

He was high up on the top floor. At one end of the corridor the window looked out over the heart of Venice, red roofs, canals, little bridges. At the other end was the Grand Canal. Guido stopped and regarded the flashing water, snaking its way through the heart of the little city to where it would reach the Palazzo Calvani, home of the Calvani counts for centuries. By tonight he might have inherited the title, and the thought appalled him.

His mercurial spirits weren't often depressed. He approached life with an optimism that was reflected in his appearance. His blue eyes might have been born gleaming, and a smile seemed to be his natural expression. At thirty-two, rich, handsome, free, he had no cares, save for the one that now threatened him.

Guido was a man of warm affections. He loved his uncle. But he also loved his freedom, and within a few hours he might have lost them both.

He turned swiftly as two young men appeared from the staircase below.

'Thank heavens!' he said, embracing his half-brother Leo, who clasped him back unselfconsciously. With his cousin Marco he merely clapped him on the shoulder. There was a proud reserve about Marco that even the open-hearted Guido had to respect.

'How bad is Uncle Francesco?' Marco demanded tersely.

'Very bad, I think. I called you last night because he'd started to have pains in his chest, but he wouldn't be sensible and see a doctor. Then early this morning he collapsed in agony, and I sent for an ambulance. We've been here ever since. They're still doing tests.'

'It surely can't be a heart attack,' Leo said. 'He's never had one before, and the life he's led—'

'Was enough to give any normal man a dozen heart attacks,' Marco supplied. 'Women, wine, fast cars—'

'Women!' Guido echoed.

'Three speedboats smashed up,' Leo recalled.

'Gambling!'

'Women!'

'Skiing!'

'Mountaineering!'

'*Women*!' They spoke with one voice.

A footstep on the stairs reduced them all to silence as Lizabetta, the count's housekeeper, appeared among them like doom. She was thin, sharp-faced, elderly, and they greeted her with more respect than they ever showed their uncle. This grim creature was the power in the Palazzo Calvani.

She acknowledged them with a nod that managed to combine respect for their aristocratic status with contempt for the male sex, sat down and took out her knitting.

'I'm afraid there's no news yet,' Guido told her gently.

He looked up as the ward door opened and the doctor emerged. He was an elderly man and had been the count's friend for years. His grave expression could mean only one thing, and their hearts sank.

The doctor pronounced. 'Get the silly old fool out of here and stop wasting my time.'

'But—his heart attack—?' Guido protested.

'Heart attack, my foot! Indigestion! Liza, you shouldn't let him eat prawns in butter.'

Liza glared. 'Much notice he takes of me,' she snapped.

'Can we see him now?' Guido asked.

A roar from within answered him. In his prime Count Francesco had been known as The Lion of Venice, and now that he was in his seventies nothing much had changed.

The three young men entered their uncle's room and stood regarding him wryly. He was sitting up in bed, his face framed by his white hair, his blue eyes gleaming.

'Gave you a fright, didn't I?' he bawled.

'Enough of a fright to bring me all the way from Rome and Leo from Tuscany,' Marco remarked. 'All because you've been stuffing yourself.'

'Don't talk to the head of the family like that,' Francesco growled. 'And blame Liza. Her cooking is irresistible.'

'So you have to gobble it like a greedy schoolboy,' Marco observed, not noticeably intimidated by addressing the head of the family. 'Uncle, when are you going to act your age?'

'I didn't get to be seventy-two by acting my age!' Francesco remarked with perfect truth. He pointed at Marco. 'When *you're* seventy-two you'll be a dried-up stick without a heart.'

Marco shrugged.

The old man indicated Leo. 'When *you're* seventy-two you'll be more of a country bumpkin than you are already.'

'That's cool,' Leo observed, unruffled.

'What will I be at seventy-two?' Guido asked.

'You won't. An outraged husband will have shot you long before then.'

Guido grinned. 'You should know all about outraged husbands, uncle. I heard that only last—'

'Clear off all of you. Liza will bring me home.'

As soon as they'd escaped the building they leaned against the honey-coloured stone wall and breathed out long sighs of relief.

'I need a drink,' Guido said, making a beeline for a small bar beside the water. The others followed him and seated themselves at a table in the sun.

Since Guido lived in Venice, Leo in Tuscany and Marco in Rome they saw each other only rarely, and the next few minutes were occupied by taking stock. Leo was the least altered. As his uncle had said, he was a countryman, lean, hard-bodied, with a candid face and clear eyes. He wasn't a subtle man. Life reached him directly, through his senses, and he read books only when necessary.

Marco was the same as always, but more so: a little more tense, a little more focused, a little more heedless of ordinary mortals. He existed in a rarefied world of high finance, and it seemed to his cousins that he was happiest there. He lived expensively, buying only the best, which he could well afford. But he did so, less because it gave him pleasure than because it would never have occurred to him to do otherwise.

Guido's mercurial nature had been born for a double life. Officially he resided at the palazzo, but he also had a discreet bachelor flat where he could come and go, free of critical eyes. He too had intensified, becoming more charming, and more elusive in his determination to remain his own man. He possessed a mulish stubbornness which he hid behind laughter and a sweet temper. His dark hair was a shade too long, curving over his collar with a slight shagginess that made him look younger than his thirty-two years.

Nobody spoke until they were on their second beer.

'I can't stand this,' Guido said at last. 'Being brought to the brink and then let off is going to finish me. And let off for how long?'

'What are you raving about?' Marco demanded.

'Ignore him,' Leo grinned. 'A man who's just been reprieved is bound to be light-headed.'

'That's right, mock me!' Guido said. 'By rights it should be you in this mess.'

Leo was his elder brother, but by a trick of fate it was Guido who was the heir. Bertrando, their father, had married a widow whose 'late' husband had subsequently turned up alive. By then she had already died giving birth to Leo, leaving him illegitimate. Two years later Bertrando had married again, and his second wife had presented him with Guido.

Nobody had worried about it then. It was a technicality that would cease to matter when Count Francesco married and had a son. But as the years passed with no sign of his marriage the anomaly began to glare. Although the younger son, Guido was legally the *only* son, and heir to the title.

He hated the prospect. It was a trap waiting to imprison his free spirit. He longed for a miracle to restore Leo's rights, but Leo didn't want them either. Only the earth interested him: growing wine, wheat and olives, breeding cattle and horses. He cared for the title no more than Guido.

The only discord between them had come when Guido tried to tempt his brother into legal action to legitimatise himself and stop 'shirking his duty'. Leo had bluntly replied that if Guido thought he was going to tie himself down to a load of pointless flapdoodle he was even more *cretino* than he looked. Guido had responded with equal robustness and it had taken Marco to stop an undignified brawl. As the son of Silvio, younger brother to Francesco and Bertrando, he had little chance of the title, and could afford to regard the shenanigans of the other two with lofty amusement.

'Of course it's bound to happen one day,' he mused now, maliciously. 'Count Guido, father of ten, a man of distinction, fat, sedate, middle-aged, with a wife to match.'

'That shirt looks like it's worth a thousand dollars,' Guido mused, fingering his half-full glass significantly.

'Only a joke,' Marco placated him.

'Not funny.' Guido took another swallow and sighed mournfully. 'Not funny at all.'

Roscoe Harrison's London home was no palace, but it had had as much money lavished on it as the Calvani abode. The difference was that he was a man without taste. He believed in display, and the crude power of cash, and it showed.

'I buy only the best,' he was saying now to the fair-haired young woman sitting in his office at the back of the house. 'That's why I'm buying you.'

'You aren't buying me, Mr Harrison,' Dulcie said coolly. 'You're hiring my skill as a private detective. There's a big difference.'

'Well your skill will do me just fine. Take a look at this.'

He thrust a photograph across the desk. It showed Roscoe's daughter, Jenny Harrison, her dark hair streaming over her shoulders in the Venetian sunlight, listening ardently to a young gondolier playing a mandolin, while another gondolier, with curly hair and a baby face, looked on.

'That's the character who thinks he's going to marry Jenny for her fortune,' Roscoe snapped, jabbing at the mandolin player with his finger. 'He's told her he isn't really a gondolier, but heir to a count—Calvani, or some such name—but I say it's a big, fat lie.

'I'm not an unreasonable man. If he really were a posh nob that would be different. His title, my money. Fair enough. But a posh nob rowing a gondola? I don't think so. I want you to go to Venice, find out what's going on. Then, when you've proved he's no aristocrat—'

'Perhaps he is,' Dulcie murmured.

Roscoe snorted. 'Your job is to prove he isn't.'

Dulcie winced. 'I can't prove he isn't if he is,' she pointed out.

'Well, you'll be able to tell, 'cos you're top drawer yourself. You're *Lady* Dulcie Maddox, aren't you?'

'In my private life, yes. But when I'm working I'm simply, Dulcie Maddox, PI.'

She guessed that Roscoe didn't like that. He was impressed by her titled connections, and when she brushed them aside he felt cheated.

Last night he'd invited her to dinner in order to meet his daughter, Jenny. Dulcie had been charmed by the young girl's freshness and naïvety. It was easy to believe that she needed protection from a fortune hunter.

'I want you because you're the best,' Roscoe returned to his theme. 'You're posh. You act posh. You look posh—not your clothes because they're—'

'Cheap,' she supplied. The jeans and denim jacket had been the cheapest thing on the market stall. Luckily she had the kind of tall, slender figure that brought out the best in anything, and her mane of fair hair and strange green eyes drew admiration wherever she went.

'Inexpensive,' Roscoe said in one of his rare ventures into tact. 'But *you* look posh, in yourself. You can tell aristocrats because they're so tall and slim. Probably comes from eating proper food while the peasants had to make do with stodge.'

'Maybe with the others,' Dulcie said. 'But with me it came from not having enough to eat because all the family money was blown on the horses. That's why I'm working as a private investigator. I'm as poor as a church mouse.'

'Then you'll need a load of new gear to be convincing. I keep an account at Feltham's for Jenny. I'll call and tell them to do you proud at my expense. When you reach the Hotel Vittorio you've got to look the part.'

'The Vittorio?' She looked quickly out of the window, lest he guess that this particular hotel had a special meaning for her. It was only a few weeks ago that she had been planning her honeymoon in that very hotel, with a man who'd sworn eternal love.

But that was then. This was now. Love had vanished with brutal suddenness. She would have given anything to avoid the Vittorio, but there was no help for it.

'Most expensive hotel in Venice,' Roscoe said. 'So buy the clothes, then get out there fast. Fly first class. No cheap economy flights in case he checks up on you.'

'You mean he might employ a private detective too?'

'No knowing. Some people are devious enough for anything.'

Dulcie maintained a diplomatic silence.

'Here's a cheque for expenses. It's not enough to look rich. You've got to splash it around a bit.'

'Splash it around a bit,' Dulcie recited, glassy eyed at the size of the cheque.

'Find this gondolier, make him think you're rolling in money, so he'll make up to you. When you've got him hooked let me know. I'll send Jenny out there, and she'll see the kind of man he really is. She won't believe it, but the world is full of jerks on the look out for a rich girl.'

'Yes,' Dulcie murmured with feeling. 'It is.'

On the night of Count Francesco's return, supper at the palazzo was formal. The four men sat around an ornate table while a maid served dish after dish, under the eagle eyes of Liza. To the count this was normal, and Marco was comfortable with it. But the other two found it suffocating, and they were glad when the meal was over.

As they prepared for escape the count signalled for Guido to join him in his ornate study.

'We'll be at *Luigi's Bar*,' Marco called back from the front door.

'Couldn't this wait?' Guido pleaded, following his uncle into the study.

'No, it can't wait,' Francesco growled. 'There are things to be said. I won't bother to ask if the stories I've heard about you are true.'

'They probably are,' Guido agreed with a grin.

'It's time it stopped. After all the trouble I've taken, making sure you met every woman in society.'

'I'm nervous with society women. They're all after just one thing!'

'*What*!'

'My future title. Half of them never look at me properly. Their gaze is fixed on the Calvani honours.'

'If you mean that they're prepared to overlook your disgraceful way of life out of respect for your dignity—'

'Dignity be blowed. Besides, maybe I don't want a woman who'll overlook my "disgraceful" life. It might be more fun if she was ready to join in.'

'Marriage is not supposed to be fun!' Francesco thundered.

'I was afraid of that.'

'It's time you started acting like a man of distinction instead of spending your time with the Lucci family, fooling about in gondolas—'

'I like rowing a gondola.'

'The Luccis are fine hard-working people but their lives take one path and yours another—'

In a flash Guido's face lost its good humour and hardened. 'The Luccis are my friends, and you'll oblige me by remembering that.'

'You can be friends—but you can't live Fede's life. You've got to make your own way. Perhaps I shouldn't have allowed you to see so much of them.'

'You didn't allow me,' Guido said quietly. 'I didn't ask your permission. Nor would I. Ever. Uncle, I have the greatest respect for you, but I won't allow you to run my life.'

When Guido spoke in that tone the merry charmer vanished, and there was something in his eyes that made even the count wary. He saw it now and fell silent. Guido was instantly contrite.

'There's no harm in it,' he said gently. 'I just like to row. It keeps me fit after my other "excesses".'

'If it were just rowing,' Francesco snorted, recovering lost ground. 'But I've heard you even sing "O sole mio" for tourists.'

'They expect it. Especially the British. It's something to do with ice cream cornets.'

'And you pose with them for photographs.' The count took out a snapshot showing Guido in gondoliering costume, serenading a pretty, dark-haired girl, while another gondolier, with curly hair and a baby face, sat just behind them.

'My nephew,' he growled, 'the future Count Calvani, *poses in a straw hat.*'

'It's disgraceful,' Guido agreed. 'I'm a blot on the family name. You'll just have to marry quickly, have a son, and cut me out. Rumour says you're still as vigorous as ever, so it shouldn't be—'

'Get out of here if you know what's good for you!'

Guido fled with relief, leaving the building and slipping away down tiny, darkened streets. As he reached the Grand Canal he saw a collection of seven gondolas, moving side by side. It was a 'serenade', a show put on to please the tourists. In the central boat the baby-faced young man from the photograph stood singing in a sweet tenor that drifted across the water. As the song came to an end there was applause, and the boats drifted in to their moorings.

Guido waited until his friend, Federico Lucci, had assisted his last passenger to disembark before hailing him.

'Hey there, Fede! If the English *signorina* could hear

you sing like that she would follow you to the ends of the earth,' he said. 'What's the matter?' for Fede had groaned. 'Doesn't she love you any more?'

'Jenny loves me,' Fede declared. 'But her Poppa will kill me before he lets us marry. He thinks I'm only after her money, but it isn't true. I love her. That time you met, didn't you think she was wonderful?'

'Wonderful,' Guido said, diplomatically concealing his opinion that Jenny was a pretty doll who lacked spice in her character. His own taste was for a woman who could offer a challenge, lead him a merry dance and give as good as she got. But he was too kind a friend to say so.

'You know I'll help in any way I can,' he said warmly.

'You've already helped us so much,' Fede said, 'letting us meet in your apartment, covering for me on the gondola—'

'That's nothing. I enjoy it. Let me know when you want me to do it again.'

'My Jenny has returned to England. She says she will reason with her Poppa, but I'm afraid she may never return.'

'If it's true love, she'll come back,' Guido insisted.

Fede gave a shout of laughter and thumped him on the shoulder. 'What do you know about true love? With you it's here-today-and-gone-tomorrow. If they mention marriage you dive for cover.'

'Sssh!' Guido looked hunted. 'My uncle has ears everywhere. Now come on, let's join Leo and Marco at *Luigi's*, and we can all get drunk in peace.'

Two days later Dulcie flew to Venice, landing at Marco Polo Airport and waiting, with an air of aloof grandeur, while her luggage was loaded onto the Vittorio's private motor launch.

It was early June, and as the boatman started the trip across the lagoon the sun was high in the sky and the light glinted on the water. Surrounded by so much bright beauty Dulcie briefly forgot her sadness.

To her right she could see the causeway linking Venice to the mainland. A train was making its way across. On the other side the lagoon stretched far away to the horizon.

'There, *signorina*,' the boatman said, speaking with the pride all Venetians feel in their city.

What she saw at first were shining orbs, gradually resolving themselves into golden cupolas, gleaming in the sun. The city itself, delicate and perfect, came gradually into view, taking her breath away with its beauty. She stayed motionless, not wanting to miss anything, as the motor boat slowed down.

'We have to enter Venice gently,' the driver explained, 'so that we do not cause any large waves. This is the Cannaregio Canal, which will take us to the Grand Canal, and the Vittorio.'

Suddenly the brightness of the lagoon was blotted out and they were drifting in shadow between high buildings. Dulcie resumed her seat and leaned back, looking up to the narrow strip of sky overhead. After a few minutes they were in sunlight again, heading down the Grand Canal to a magnificent seventeenth-century palace. The Hotel Vittorio.

At the landing-stage hands reached down to help her up the steps and guide her into the hotel. She made a stately entrance, followed by porters bearing her luggage in procession.

'The Empress Suite,' declared a lofty individual on the desk.

'The Emp—?' she echoed, dismayed. 'Are you sure there hasn't been a mistake?'

But she was already being swept away to the third floor where gilded double doors opened before her and she walked into the palatial apartment. Everything about it was designed to look like the abode of an empress, including the eighteenth-century furniture. On one wall hung a portrait of the beautiful, young Empress Elisabeth of Austria, painted in the nineteenth century when Venice had been an Austrian province.

To one side was another pair of double doors, through which Dulcie found her bedroom, with a bed large enough to sleep four. She gasped, overwhelmed by such opulence. A maid appeared, ready to unpack her luggage. Just in time she remembered Roscoe's orders to 'splash it about a bit' and distributed tips large enough to get herself talked about even in this place.

When everyone had gone she sat in silence, trying to come to terms with the shock of being here, alone, when she should have been here as a blissful bride.

She forced herself to confront the memory of Simon, painful though it was. He'd assumed that *Lady* Dulcie Maddox, daughter of Lord Maddox, must have a potful of family money hidden somewhere. He'd courted her ardently, using practised words to sweep her away in a magic balloon, to a place where everything was love and gratification.

But the balloon had fallen to earth, with her in it.

Simon had lived lavishly—all on credit, as she'd later discovered. She hadn't cared about his money, only about his love. But the one was as illusory as the other.

He'd shown her the Hotel Vittorio's brochure one

evening when they were dining at the Ritz. 'I've already made our honeymoon booking,' he'd said, 'in the Empress Suite.'

'But darling, the cost—'

'So what? Money is for spending.'

She'd spoken with passionate tenderness. 'You don't have to spend a lot on me. Money isn't what it's about.'

His quizzical frown should have warned her. 'No, sweetie, but it helps.'

Then she'd said—and the memory tormented her still— 'You don't think I'm marrying you for your money do you? I love you, *you*. I wouldn't care if you were as poor as I am.'

She could still see the wary look that came into his eyes, and sense the chill that settled over him. 'This is a wind up, right? As poor as Lady Dulcie Maddox.'

'You can't eat a title. I haven't a penny.'

'I heard your grandfather blew twenty grand at the races in one day.'

'That's right. And my father was the same. That's *why* I haven't a penny.'

'But you lot have all got trust funds, everyone knows that.'

The truth had got through to her now, but she fought not to face it. 'Do I live like someone with a trust fund?'

'Go on, you're just slumming.'

She'd finally convinced him that she wasn't, and that was the last time she saw him. Her final memory was of him snatching a credit card statement from his pocket and tossing it at her with the bitter words, 'Do you know how much money I've spent on you? And for what? Well, no more.'

Then he stormed out of the Ritz, leaving her to pay for the meal.

And that had been that.

Sitting in the quiet of the Empress Suite Dulcie knew that it was time to pull herself together. Now there was another fortune hunter, but this time he was the prey and she the pursuer, seeking him out for retribution, the avenger of all women.

She showered in a gold and marble bathroom and chose something to wear for her first outing 'on duty'. She finally left the hotel arrayed in an orange silk dress, with a delicate pendant of pure gold. Gold earrings and dainty gilt sandals completed the ensemble. So much gold might be overdoing it, but she needed to make an impression, fast.

When she'd finished she took a final look at the picture, to make sure his face was imprinted on her mind. She dismissed the baby-faced boy at the back. There was the one she wanted, playing the mandolin, overflowing with confidence, smiling at Jenny, no doubt serenading her with honeyed words. The rat!

Finding one gondolier among so many was a problem, but she'd come prepared. Guidebooks had told her about the *vaporetto*, the great water buses that transported passengers along the Grand Canal, so she headed for one of the landing stages, boarded the next boat, and took up a position in the front, armed with powerful binoculars.

For an hour the *vaporetto* moved along the canal, criss-crossing to landing stages on each side, while Dulcie searched for her quarry, without success. At the end of the line she turned back and started again. No luck this time either, and she was almost about to give up when suddenly she saw him.

It was only a glimpse, too brief to be sure, but there was the gondola gliding between two buildings while she frantically focused the binoculars, catching him clearly only at the last moment.

The *vaporetto* was about to cast off from a landing stage. Dulcie moved fast, jumping ashore just in time and looking desperately about her. The gondola had vanished. She plunged down an alley between tall buildings to a small canal at the far end. No sign of him there, but he must be somewhere to her left. She made for a tiny bridge, tore over it and into another dark alley.

At the far end was another small canal, another bridge. A gondola was heading towards her. But was it the same one? The gondolier's face was hidden by a straw hat. She placed herself on the bridge, watching intently as the long boat neared, the oarsman standing at the far end.

'Lift your head,' she agonised. 'Look *up*!'

He had almost reached the bridge. In a moment it would be too late. Driven by desperation she wrenched off one of her shoes and tossed it over the side. It struck his hat, knocking it off, before landing exactly at his feet.

Then he looked up, and there was the face she'd come to Venice seeking, the face of the mandolin player. Eyes of fierce, startling blue, set in a laughing face, seemed to seize her, hold her, almost hypnotise her, so that she found herself smiling back.

'*Buon giorno, bella signorina,*' said Guido Calvani.

CHAPTER TWO

No SOONER were the words out of his mouth than he'd vanished under the bridge. Dulcie dashed to the other side as he emerged and began to negotiate his way to the shore. She took a quick look at the picture to make sure she had the right man. Yes, there he was, smiling at Jenny, playing the mandolin.

Thank goodness he didn't have a passenger, she thought as she hobbled off the bridge and along to where he'd pulled in.

'I'm so sorry,' she called. 'I just turned my foot and the shoe slid off and went right over the side of the bridge before I could grab it. And then it hit you on the head. I'll never forgive myself if you're hurt.'

He grinned, holding up the dainty gilt sandal with its absurdly high heel.

'But I am hurt, very badly. Not in my head but—' he bowed gallantly with his hand over his heart.

This was what she'd expected. Practised charm. Right! She was ready for him.

He'd pulled in by a short flight of steps that ran down into the water.

'If you will sit down, I'll return this to you in the proper fashion,' he said.

She sat on the top step and felt her ankle grasped in strong, warm fingers as he slid the shoe back onto her foot, adjusting it precisely.

'Thank you—Federico.'

He gave a little start. 'Fed—?'

'It's written there.' Dulcie pointed to a label stitched near his collar, bearing the name Federico.

'Oh, yes, of course,' Guido said hurriedly. He'd forgotten Fede's mother's habit of sewing nametapes on the gondolier shirts of her husband, two brothers and three sons. No matter. He would simply tell her his real name. But he became distracted by the feel of her dainty ankle in his palm, and when he looked up he found her watching him with a quizzical look that drove everything else out of his mind. What did names matter?

'And you are new to Venice?' he asked.

'I arrived only today.'

'Then you must accept my apologies for your rough introduction to my city. But let me say also that the stones of Venice will not be kind to those shoes.'

'It wasn't very bright of me to wear such high heels, was it?' she asked, looking shamefaced. 'But I didn't know, you see. Venice is so different to anywhere else in the world, and there's nobody to tell me anything.' She managed to sound a little forlorn.

'That's terrible,' he said sympathetically. 'For a beautiful young lady to be alone is always a shame, but to be alone in Venice is a crime against nature.'

He said it so delightfully, she thought. Lucky for her she was armed in advance.

'I'd better go back to my hotel and change into sensible shoes before I have another accident.' She became aware that his fingers were still clasped about her ankle. 'Would you mind?'

'Forgive me.' He snatched back his hand. 'May I take you to your hotel?'

'But I thought gondoliers didn't do that. Surely you only do round trips?'

'It's true that we don't act like taxis. But in your case

I would like to make an exception. Please—' He was holding out his hand. She placed her own hand in it and rose to her feet, then let him help her down the steps to the water.

'Steady,' he said, helping her into the well of the gondola, which rocked, forcing her to clutch him for safety.

'You sit here,' he said, settling into the rear-facing seats, an arrangement that would enable him to see her face. 'It's better if you don't face the front,' he hurriedly improvised. 'At this hour people get the setting sun in their eyes. And you might get seasick,' he added for good measure.

'I'll do just as you say,' she agreed demurely. She supposed she could be blinded by the setting sun from either direction, depending on which route he took, but she appreciated his strategy.

It suited her, too, to be able to lean back and stretch out her long, silk-clad legs before his gaze. True, she was supposed to be tempting him with the prospect of money, but there was no harm in using the weapons nature had bestowed.

He cast off, and for a while they went gently through narrow canals, where buildings rose sheer out of the water. They glided under a bridge and as it slid away she saw that it seemed to emerge direct from one building, over the water and straight into another. Dulcie watched in wonder, beginning to understand how this city was truly different from all others.

He was a clever man, she thought. He knew better than to spoil it by talking. Only the soft splash of his oar broke the silence, and gradually a languor came over her. Already Venice was casting its spell, bidding her forget everything but itself, and give herself up to floating through beauty.

'It's another world,' she murmured. 'Like something that fell to earth from a different planet.'

An arrested look came into his eyes. 'Yes,' he said. 'That's exactly it.'

They seemed to drift for ages, one beauty crowding on the last, too many impressions for her to sort them out. Vaguely she remembered that this wasn't why she was here. Her job was to work on the man standing there, guiding twenty-two feet of heavy, curved wood as though it was the easiest thing in the world.

She considered him, and found that she understood why a naïve, sheltered girl like Jenny found him irresistible. He was tall, not heavily built but with a wiry strength that she'd already felt when he'd helped her into the boat. Just a light gesture, but the steel had been there, unmistakable, exciting. He handled the heavy oar as though it weighed nothing, moving with it, lithe and graceful, as though they were dancing partners.

They passed into a wider canal, and suddenly the sun was on him. Dulcie looked up, shading her eyes against the glare, and at once he removed his straw boater and tossed it to her.

'You wear it,' he called. 'The sun is hot.'

She rammed it onto her head and leaned back, taking pleasure in the way the light illuminated his throat and the strong column of his neck, and touched off a hint of red in his hair. How intensely blue his eyes were, she thought, and how naturally they crinkled at the corners when he smiled. And he smiled easily. He was doing so now, his head on one side as though inviting her to share a joke, so that she couldn't help joining in with his laughter.

'Are we nearly there?' she asked.

'There?' he asked with beguiling innocence. 'Where?'

'At my hotel.'

'But you didn't tell me which hotel.'

'And you didn't ask me. So how do we know we're going in the right direction?'

His shrug was a masterpiece, asking if it really mattered. And it didn't.

Dulcie pulled herself together. She was supposed to toss the hotel name at him, advertising her 'wealth'. Instead she'd revelled in the magic of his company for—good heavens, *an hour*?

'The Hotel Vittorio,' she said firmly.

He didn't react, but of course, he wouldn't, she reasoned. A practised seducer would know better than to seem impressed.

'It's an excellent hotel, *signorina*,' he said. 'I hope you are enjoying it.'

'Well, the Empress Suite is a little overwhelming,' she said casually, just to drive the point home.

'And very sad, for a lady alone,' he pointed out. 'But perhaps you have friends who'll soon move into the second bedroom.'

'You know the Empress Suite?'

'I've seen the inside,' Guido said vaguely. It was true. His friends from America regularly stayed there, and he'd downed many a convivial glass in those luxurious surroundings.

I'll bet you've seen the inside, Dulcie thought, getting her cynicism back safely into place.

'When your friends arrive you'll feel better,' he said.

'There are no friends. I'm spending this vacation on my own.' They were pulling in to the Vittorio's landing stage, and he reached out to help her onto land. 'How much do I owe you?' she asked.

'Nothing.'

'But of course I must pay you. I've had an hour of your time.'

'Nothing,' he repeated, and she felt his hand tighten on her wrist. 'Please don't insult me with money.' His eyes were very blue, holding hers, commanding her to do what he wished.

'I didn't mean to insult you,' she said slowly. 'It's just that—'

'It's just that money pays for everything,' he finished. 'But only if it is for sale.' He spoke with sudden intensity. 'Don't be alone in Venice. That's bad.'

'I don't have a choice.'

'But you do. Let me show you my city.'

'Your city?'

'Mine because I love it and know its ways as no stranger can. I would like you to love it too.'

It was on the tip of her tongue to make one of the flirtatious replies she'd been practising for just this moment, but the words wouldn't come. She had a sense of being at the point of no return. To go on was risky and there would be no way back. But to withdraw was to spend a lifetime wondering 'what if?'

'I don't think—' she said slowly. 'I don't think I should.'

'I think you should,' he said urgently.

'But—'

His hand tightened on hers. 'You *must*. Don't you know that you must?'

The glow of his eyes was almost fierce in its intensity. She drew a sharp breath. She didn't come from a long line of gamblers for nothing.

'Yes,' she said. 'I must.'

'I'll meet you at seven o'clock at *Antonio's*. It's just around the corner. And wear walking shoes.'

She watched as he glided away, then hurried up to her suite, glad of the time alone to gather her thoughts.

It wasn't easy. In a few blazing moments he'd taken her ideas and tossed them into the air, so that they'd fallen about her in disorder. It took some stern concentration to reclaim her mind from his influence, but at last she felt she'd managed it.

Stage one completed successfully. Quarry identified, contact made. Ground laid for stage two. Professional detachment. Never forget that.

Guido got away from the hotel as fast as he could before he was spotted by someone who knew his true identity. In a few minutes he'd left the city centre behind and was heading for the little back 'streets' in the northern part of town, where the gondolier families lived, and their boatyards flourished.

At the Lucci house he found Federico at home watching a football match on television. Without a word he took a beer from the fridge and joined him, neither speaking until half time. Then, as he always did, Guido put the money he'd earned on the table, nearly doubling it with extra from his own pocket.

'I had a good day, didn't I?' Fede said appreciatively, pocketing the money with a yawn.

'Excellent. You're an example to us all.'

'At this rate I think I've earned a holiday.'

'I know *I* have.' Guido rubbed his arms, which were aching.

'Perhaps it's time you got back to the souvenir trade.'

Guido had established his independence of the

Calvani family by setting up his own business, catering to tourists. He owned two factories on the outlying island of Murano, one of which made glass, and the other trinkets and souvenirs.

'I suppose it is,' he said now, unenthusiastically. 'It's just that—Fede, have you ever found yourself doing something you never meant to do—just a word, a choice to be made in a split second? And suddenly your whole life has changed?'

'Sure. When I met my Jenny.'

'And you don't know how it's all going to end, but you do know that you have to go on and find out?'

Fede nodded. 'That's just how it is.'

'So what do I do?'

'My friend, you've already supplied the answer. I don't know what's happened, but I do know it's too late for you to turn back.'

An important decision demanded long, serious deliberation, so when Dulcie opened the palatial wardrobe to select something suitable for the coming evening she went through the multitude of dresses with great care.

'How did I ever buy all this?' she murmured.

She'd gone to Feltham's, as instructed, and found the staff already primed with Roscoe's demands. As these would have resulted in her looking like a Christmas tree Dulcie had waved them aside and insisted on her own kind of discreet elegance. After four outfits she tried to call a halt, but the superior person assigned to assist her was horrified.

'Mr Harrison said the bill must be at least twenty thousand,' she'd murmured.

'Twenty thou—? He can wear them then.'

'He'll be most displeased if we don't live up to his expectations. It could cost me my job.'

Put like that, it became a duty to spend money, and by the time she'd left the luxury store she was the owner of five cocktail dresses, two glamorous evening gowns, three pairs of designer jeans, any number of designer sweaters, a mountain of silk and satin underwear, and a collection of summer dresses. Some expensive make-up and perfume, plus several items of luggage completed the list.

She surveyed her booty now, hanging in the hotel's luxurious, air-conditioned closets, in a mood of ironic depression. This ought to have been a fun job, the chance to be Cinderella at the ball. If only it hadn't been Venice, and if only the high life she was to lead hadn't been so much like the life her Prince Charmless had expected of her.

Why had she accepted *this* assignment, in a place where every sight and sound would hurt her. Was she mad?

Then she set her chin. This was a chance to make a man pay for his crimes against women. She must never forget that.

She took so long making her choice that she was late when she finally hurried downstairs wearing a cocktail dress of pale-blue silk organza with silver filigree accessories. Her silver shoes had heels of only one inch, which was the nearest she could get to 'sensible'.

Antonio's was a tiny place with tables outside, sheltered by a leaf-hung trellis. It looked charming, but there was something missing. Him!

No matter, he'd be inside. She sauntered in, looking casual, but her air of indifference fell away as she saw no sign of him here either.

He'd stood her up!

It was the one thing she hadn't thought of.

Be reasonable, she thought. He's just a few minutes late—like you.

That's different, replied her awkward self. He's supposed to be trying to seduce me, and he can't even be bothered to do it properly.

Setting her jaw she marched out and collided with a man hurtling himself through the door in the other direction.

'*Mio dio!*' Guido exploded in passionate relief. 'I thought you'd stood me up.'

'*I*—?'

'When you didn't come I thought you'd changed your mind. I've been looking for you.'

'I was only ten minutes late,' she protested.

'Ten minutes, ten hours? It felt like forever. I suddenly realised that I don't know your name. You might have vanished and how could I have found you again? But I've found you now.' He took her hand. 'Come with me.'

He was walking away, drawing her behind him, before she could stop and think that once more he'd reversed their roles, so that he was now giving orders. But she followed him, eager to see where he would lead her, and curiously content in his company.

He'd changed out of his working clothes into jeans and a shirt of such snowy whiteness that it gave him an air of elegance, and made a contrast with his lightly tanned skin.

'You could have found me quite easily,' she pointed out as they strolled hand in hand. 'You know my hotel.'

'To be sure, I could go into the Vittorio and say the lady in their best suite has given me the elbow and would they please tell me her name? Then I think I should start running before they throw me out. They're used to dealing with dodgy characters.'

'Are you a dodgy character?' she asked with interest.

'They'd certainly think so if I told them that tale. Now where shall we go?'

'You're the one who knows Venice.'

'And from the depths of my expert knowledge I say that we should start with an ice cream.'

'Yes please,' she said at once. There was something about ice cream that made a child of her again. He picked up the echo and grinned boyishly.

'Come on.'

He led her into a maze, where streets and canals soon blurred into one. Flagstones underfoot, alleys so narrow that the old buildings almost seemed to touch each other overhead, tiny bridges where they lingered to watch the boats drift underneath.

'It's all so peaceful,' she said in wonder.

'That's because there are no cars.'

'Of course.' She looked around her. 'I hadn't even realised, but it's obvious.' She looked around her again. 'There's nowhere for cars to go.'

'Right,' he said with deep satisfaction. 'Nowhere at all. They can leave the mainland and come out over the causeway as far as the terminal. But then people have to get out and walk. If they don't want to walk they go by boat. But they don't bring their smelly, stinking cars into my city.'

'Your city? You keep saying that.'

'Every true Venetian speaks of Venice as his city. He pretends that he owns it, to hide the fact that it owns him. It's a possessive mother who won't release him. Wherever he goes in the world this perfect place goes with him, holding onto him, drawing him back.' He stopped himself with an awkward laugh. 'Now Venice thinks we should go and eat ice cream.'

He took her to a small café by a little canal so quiet that the world might have forgotten it. He summoned a waiter, talking to him in a language Dulcie didn't recognise, and making expansive gestures, while giving her a look of wicked mischief.

'Were you speaking Italian?' she asked when they were alone again.

'Venetian dialect.'

'It sounds like a different language to Italian.'

'In effect it is.'

'It's a bit hard on tourists who learn a bit of Italian for their vacation, and then find you speaking Venetian.'

'We speak Italian and English for the tourists, but amongst ourselves we speak our dialect because we are *Venetian*.'

'Like a another country,' she said thoughtfully.

'Of course. Venice was once an independent republic, not just a province of Italy, but a state in its own right. And that's still how we feel. That is our pride, to be Venetian first, before all other allegiances.'

As before, there was a glow on his face that told her he felt passionately about this subject. She began to watch him intently, eager to hear more, but suddenly the waiter appeared with their order, and he fell silent. She had a sense of let-down, and promised herself that she would draw him back to this subject later.

She understood her companion's mischievous expression when two huge dishes of vanilla and chocolate ice cream were brought to the table, plus two jugs, one containing chocolate sauce and one containing cream.

'I ordered chocolate because it's my favourite,' he explained.

'Suppose it isn't mine?'

'Don't worry, I'll finish it for you.'

She gave an involuntary choke of laughter, and bit it back, remembering the aloof role she was supposed to be playing. But she made the mistake of meeting his eyes, daring her not to laugh, so that she had to give in.

'Now tell me your name,' he insisted.

'It's—Dulcie.' She was mysteriously reluctant to say the rest.

'Only Dulcie?'

'Lady Dulcie Maddox.'

He raised his eyebrows. 'An aristocrat?'

'A very minor one.'

'But you have a title?'

'My father has the title. He's an earl. In Italy he would be a count.'

A strange look came over his face. 'A—count?' he echoed slowly. 'You are the daughter of a count?'

'Of an earl. Does it matter?'

She had the odd impression that he pulled himself together. 'Of course you didn't want to tell me that. I understand.'

'What do you understand?' she demanded, nettled.

He shrugged. 'Dulcie can do as she pleases, but *Lady* Dulcie can't let a gondolier think he picked her up.'

'You didn't pick me up,' she said, feeling uneasy, since she could hardly admit that she'd come here to pick *him* up. 'I don't care how we got to know each other. I'm just glad that we did.'

'So am I because—because I have many things I

want to say to you. But I can't say them now. It's too soon.'

'It's too soon for you to know you want to say them.'

He shook his head. 'Oh, no,' he said quietly, 'It's not too soon for that.'

CHAPTER THREE

'You must forgive me if I talk too much about Venice,' he said. 'I forget that everyone must feel the same about their own home town.'

'I don't know,' she said thoughtfully. 'I can't imagine feeling like that about London.'

'That's where you live?'

'It is now, but I was raised on my father's estate—'

'Ah yes, Poppa the earl. And he has huge ancestral acres, yes?'

'Huge,' she agreed, mentally editing out the mortgages.

'So you were raised in the country?' he encouraged her.

'Yes, and I remember how peaceful it was there too. I used to sit by my bedroom window at dawn and watch the trees creeping out of the mist. I'd pretend they were friendly giants who could only visit me in the half-light, and I'd write stories in my head about the things they did—' she stopped and shrugged, embarrassed to have been lured into self-revelation.

But he was looking at her with interest. 'Go on,' he said.

She began to talk about her home, the childhood she'd spent there, and the imaginary friends she'd created, for her only sibling was a brother too much older than herself to be any fun. Soon she forgot all else except the pleasure of talking to someone who appeared absorbed in what she had to say. None of her family had the remotest sympathy with her 'dreaming', and at last she'd given it up in favour of good sense. Or so she'd told herself. Now she began to wonder if this side of herself had merely gone underground, to be brought back to life with the perfect listener on the perfect evening.

At some point he paid for the ice cream and took her arm to lead her out, murmuring about eating the next part of the meal elsewhere. But he did it without taking his attention from her, or interrupting the flow, and when she found herself crossing a bridge a few minutes later she wasn't quite sure how she'd arrived there.

He found another restaurant and ordered without asking her. That was how she discovered 'Venetian oysters', the shells stuffed with caviar with pepper and lemon juice, served on ice with brown bread and butter. It was ten times as good as the splendid meal served in Roscoe's house, prepared by his expensive chef. Her companion read her face, and grinned.

'We do the best cooking in the world,' he asserted without a trace of modesty.

'I believe you, I believe you,' she said fervently. 'This is pure heaven.'

'You don't mind my ordering for you?'

She shook her head. 'I wouldn't know what to ask for anyway.'

'Then you place yourself totally in my hands. *Bene!*'

'I didn't exactly say that,' she protested. 'I said you could choose the food.'

'Since we're eating, that's the same thing.'

'Well, I'm on my guard. I've heard about gondoliers,' she teased.

'And what exactly have you heard?' he was teasing her back.

'That you're a bunch of Romeos—'

'Not Romeos, Casanovas,' he corrected her seriously.

'Does it make a difference?' she asked, wondering if it was ever possible to disconcert this madman.

'Of course. This is Casanova's city. In the Piazza San Marco you can still see Florian's, the coffee-house where he used to go. Also he was imprisoned in Venice. So, you were saying—'

'You mean I can finish now?'

He placed a finger over his mouth. 'Not another word.'

'I don't believe you. Where was I?'

'We're all Casanovas—'

'Who count the girls as they come off the planes.'

'But of course we do,' he agreed shamelessly. 'Because we're always looking for the one perfect one.'

'Phooey! Who cares about perfection if it's only for a few days?'

'I always care about perfection. It matters.'

He wasn't joking any more and she was impelled to reply seriously. 'But everything can't be perfect. The world is full of imperfection.'

'Of course. That's why perfection matters. But you must know how to seek it in the little things as well as the great. Look out there.'

He pointed through the window to where the sun was setting exactly between two high buildings, looking like a stream of gold descending into the earth.

'Do you think the architect knew he was achieving exactly that perfect effect when he created those buildings?' he asked her. 'It seems fantastic, but I like to believe that he did. Perfection is where you find it.'

'Or where you think you've found it. Sometimes you must discover that you're wrong.'

'Yes,' he said after a moment. 'And then nothing looks quite the same again.' Then his laughter broke out again. 'Why are we being so serious? That comes later.'

'Oh, really? You've got our conversation all mapped out then?'

'I think we're travelling a well-worn path, you and I.'

'I'm not going to ask you which path. It might mean getting too serious again, and I'm here for fun.'

He regarded her quizzically. 'Are you saying that's why you came to Venice—looking for a holiday romance?'

'No, I—' Absurdly, the question caught her off-guard. 'No, that's not why.'

'What's the matter?' he asked at once. 'Have I said something to hurt you?

'No, of course not.'

It was hard because this man was shrewder and subtler than she had allowed for. His eyes were warm and concerned, studying her anxiously, but she needed to evade them, lest they looked too deep.

'That was lovely,' she said, indicating her empty plate. 'What have you decided on now?'

'*Polastri Pini e Boni,*' he declared at once.

'And that is—?' She was searching the menu for enlightenment. 'I can't find it.'

'It's chicken, stuffed with herbs, cheese and almonds. You won't find it on the menu. They don't do it here.'

'Then—?'

'I'm going to take you to a place where they do serve it.'

'Are we going to have every course in a different place?' she asked, slightly giddy at the thought.

'Of course. It's the ideal way to eat. Come on.'

As soon as they were outside she became completely lost. Now they were far off the tourist track, plunging into narrow, flagstoned streets that she knew were called *calle*. High overhead the last of the daylight was almost blocked out by washing strung between buildings, across the street.

'I thought all the streets were water,' she observed as they strolled along, not hurrying.

'No, there are plenty of places where it's possible to walk, but sooner or later one always comes to water.'

'But why build it like this in the first place?'

'Many centuries ago, my ancestors were running from their enemies. They fled the mainland, out into the lagoon where there were a mass of tiny islands, and they settled there. They drove stakes deep into the water to create foundations, built bridges between the islands, and so created a unity that became a city.'

'You mean this canal beneath us—' they were crossing a small bridge '—was the seaway between two separate islands? It's only about twelve feet wide.'

'They were miracle workers. And a miracle is what they created.'

'But how? It just—just defies all the laws of architecture, of science, of common sense—'

'Oh, common sense—' he said dismissively.

'I believe in it,' she said defiantly.

'Then heaven help you! It means nothing. It creates nothing, it's the opposite of a miracle. Look about you. As you say, Venice defies common sense, and yet it exists.'

'I can't deny that.'

'So much for common sense! Never resort to it again. It's the root of all the troubles in the world.'

'I'm afraid I can't help it,' she confessed. 'I grew up sensible, reliable, practical—'

He put his hands over his ears. 'Stop, stop!' he begged. 'I can't bear any more of these dreadful words. I must feed you quickly and make you well again.'

He hustled her down some steps and into a door that was almost hidden in shadows. Behind it was a tiny restaurant which was almost full despite the fact that it seemed to be in hiding. One taste of the chicken was enough to explain this contradiction. If the last course had brought her to the gates of heaven, this one ushered her through.

Guido watched her with pleasure, intent on weaving a spell around her. He wanted her securely in his magic net before he was ready to reveal certain things about himself. He was an honest man, with a high regard for the truth, but he knew that truth wasn't always reached by sticking too rigidly to the facts.

Then, as if making his very thoughts tangible, a hand clapped him on the shoulder and a cheerful voice said, 'Hey, Guido! Fancy seeing you here!'

It was Alberto, a friend and employee, who managed his glass factory, more than slightly tipsy, full of good cheer, and about to blow his cover.

Guido tensed and his glance flew to Dulcie who was mercifully absorbed in feeding a kitten that had appeared under their table. She hadn't heard Alberto call him Guido but disaster was approaching fast. The one ray of hope was that Alberto was speaking in Venetian. Grabbing his friend's wrist Guido muttered in the same language.

'Hello, old friend. Do me a favour. Get lost.'

'That's not very friendly Gui—'

'I'm not feeling friendly. Now be a good fellow and take yourself off.'

Alberto stared, then he caught sight of Dulcie and his expression cleared. 'Aha! A beautiful lady. You devil. Let me make her acquaintance.'

'You'll make the acquaintance of the canal in a minute.' Guido's smile never wavered as he uttered this half-serious threat.

'Hey, all right!' Alberto became placating, backing off. 'If it's like that—'

'I'm warning you—another word—'

'Fine, I'm going.'

Guido watched him depart, feeling as if he'd aged ten years. He should have taken Dulcie to some place where nobody knew him, but where, in Venice, was he to find such a place?

Problems crowded in on him. Soon he must tell her of his innocent deception, but how to do it needed a lot of thought. Never mind. He would 'tap-dance' his way out of that problem when the time came. He was good at that because to a warm-hearted man with a tangled personal life tap-dancing was a necessary skill.

'If you've finished, let's walk again,' he said. 'Venice will have changed.'

She saw what he meant as they stepped outside. Night had created a different city. Little alleys that had led to mysterious corners now vanished into total darkness, and lights glittered like jewels reflected in the black water. He led her onto a small bridge and stood back, letting her drink in the beauty in her own way, in peace.

Already there were a thousand things he wanted to say to her, but he held back, fearful of breaking the

spell by going too fast. He could wait, and let Venice
do its work for him.

Dulcie watched and listened, entranced. Faintly, in
the distance, she could hear the sound of mandolins,
and occasionally a strange, soft, eerie yodel.

'Whatever is that sound?'

'It's the cry a gondolier gives as he approaches a
corner,' he said. 'With twenty-two feet of boat in front
of him he has to warn any traffic crossing his path,
otherwise they'd be colliding all the time.'

As he spoke there was another yodel close by, and
the prow of a gondola appeared around the corner, turning into the canal and heading for them. Dulcie leaned
over the bridge, watching the boat with its young lovers
clasped in an embrace. Slowly they drew apart, their
faces illuminated by the lights from the bridge.

Dulcie felt a cold hand clutch her stomach. The
man—it couldn't be—she was imagining things. As the
gondola glided beneath she rushed to the other side of
the bridge in a vain attempt to see better. But that was
worse. There was only the back of his head. Perversely
this only increased her conviction that she'd seen
Simon.

A rich bride, a honeymoon in Venice, these were the
things he'd wanted. But it was only four months since
they'd parted. Could he have replaced one bride with
another so fast? Suddenly she'd moved back in time to
a turmoil of pain, disillusion, rejection, mistrust.

'Dulcie, what is it?'

She felt strong hands seize her, turn her. His face was
dark.

'Tell me what's the matter.'

'Nothing.'

'That man—you knew him—'

'No—I thought I did, but it couldn't have been him, not so soon—not here of all places—I don't know, I don't want to talk about it.'

'I see,' he said slowly. 'It's like that.'

'You don't know what it's like,' she cried angrily. 'You don't know anything.'

'You loved him, and you thought you would be here with him. That much is obvious. And it wasn't so very long ago. So perhaps you love him still?'

'It wasn't him,' she said, trying to sound firm. 'Just someone else who looked a bit like him.'

'But you're avoiding my question. Do you still love him? Or don't you know?'

'Yes—no—I don't know. I don't know anything.'

'Were you coming to Venice for your honeymoon?'

'Yes,' she sighed.

'And now you come here alone—to think of what might have been?'

That did it.

'Rubbish!' she said trenchantly. 'Absolute codswallop! How dare you suggest that I'm some sort of—of—I don't know, some sort of forlorn maiden trailing in the shadow of a dead love. Of all the sentimental drivel I ever heard—I've a good mind to—'

How he laughed. '*Brava*! *Brava*! I knew you were stronger than that. Whatever he did to you, you won't be crushed. Don't get mad, get even! Shall we follow and tip him into the water?'

'Don't be idiotic,' she said, joining in his laughter unwillingly. 'I don't even know that it's him.'

'Let's tip him in the water anyway,' he suggested hopefully.

'You clown. Whatever for?'

'As a warning to all men to be careful how they treat women in future.'

'Let's forget him,' she said hastily. She didn't know what wicked imp had made him voice the very idea that had brought her here, but it was something she couldn't afford to think of just now.

'Yes, let's forget him and plan what we shall do tomorrow. There's so much I want to show you—'

'What about your gondola? It's your living.'

'Not tomorrow. Tomorrow I forget work and think only of you.'

'Oh, really,' she teased. 'Suppose I have other ideas?'

He looked crestfallen. 'There's another man you'd rather spend the day with?'

'No, I—' she bit back the rest, realising that she'd walked into a trap.

'You'd rather spend the day with me than any other man?' he said at once. '*Bene*! That's what I hoped.'

'You're twisting my words. Maybe I want to spend the day alone.'

'Do you?'

He wasn't teasing any more, and neither was she.

'No,' she said quietly.

'We could go to the seaside, if you like?'

'Does it have a really sandy beach?' she asked longingly.

'I promise you a really sandy beach. Venice doesn't just have the best cooking in the world, it also has the best beach in the world.'

'Anything else?'

'The best swimming, and the best company. Me.'

He was laughing again, playing the jester, inviting her to mock him. Then suddenly he drew her into his arms, holding her close, but not kissing her, content just to embrace. He drew back a little and touched her face with his hands, brushing back stray tendrils of hair, and studying her intently.

'Dulcie,' he whispered. 'There's so much—but not now—this isn't the right time.'

A tremor of alarm went through her. This was too sweet, too delightful. What was she thinking of?

'I can't,' she said. 'I can't see you tomorrow.'

'Then the next day—'

'No, I can't see you again,' she said desperately. 'I'm going home. I should never have come here. Please let me go.'

He made no attempt to hold onto her as she broke free and began to run down the nearest *calle*. She simply had to get away from what was happening here. It shocked and confused her. Nothing was going according to plan.

Her footsteps slowed, then halted. It looked the same in all directions, and she had no idea where she was. By the one lamp she groped in her bag for a map and tried to work out which way up it went. It was hopeless.

'Now I'm totally lost,' she groaned.

'Not while I'm here,' he said, appearing from nowhere. 'I'll take you to the hotel. It isn't very far.'

It seemed to her that they had come for miles, but when he'd led her through *calle* after *calle*, all looking the same, she found herself near the hotel, and realised that they'd only been walking for ten minutes.

'There it is, just ahead,' he told her. 'You don't need my help any more.' He was keeping back in the shadows.

'Then I'll say goodbye,' she said, holding out her hand. 'Thank you for a lovely evening. I'm sorry it all ended so abruptly—'

'Has it "all ended"?'

'Yes, it has to. Because you see—I can't seem to get my head straight.'

'Nor mine. But my response would be the opposite of yours.'

'I'm going home tomorrow,' she said quickly. 'I really must—I can't explain but I shouldn't have come here—goodbye.'

The last word came out in a rush. Then she walked away fast, and hurried into the hotel without looking back at him.

As she opened the door of the Empress Suite her mind was functioning like an investigator's again. Cool. Calm. Collected. She was a rational thinking machine.

And the sooner she was out of here the better.

The phone rang. She knew who it would be.

'Please don't leave,' came his voice.

'I—ought to.'

'You should never do what you ought. It's a big mistake.'

'Why?' she asked, knowing that she was crazy to ask.

'Because you really ought to be doing something else.'

'That's just clever words.'

'Now you're indulging in common sense,' he reproved her. 'You must stop that.'

'More clever words.'

'You're right. Actions are better. I'll be waiting for you at ten tomorrow morning, at the *vaporetto* landing stage near the hotel. Come prepared for swimming.'

'But—'

'Ten o'clock. Don't be late.'

He hung up.

She couldn't think what was happening here. She

should be in control, but suddenly everything was out of her hands. To help collect her thoughts she went out onto her balcony and looked down the Grand Canal. It was quiet now and just a few lamps glowed in the darkness. Now and then a gondola, empty but for the silent oarsman, drifted across the water like a ghost, gliding home.

She had called the evening magic, a word which troubled her practical mind. And staying practical was essential she thought, beginning to argue with him in her mind. Let him say what he liked. She wasn't to be tricked by pretty words.

But out here, in the shadows and the cool night air, the magic couldn't be denied. Awed, she watched as one by one the café lights went out, and the water lay at peace under the moon. Still she stayed, not wanting this night to be over.

The shrill of the telephone blasted her gentle dream. It was Roscoe.

'How are you doing?' he demanded without preamble. 'Have you got anywhere yet?'

'I only arrived today,' she protested.

'You mean you haven't managed to meet him?'

'Yes, I have—'

'Great! And he's a real creep, right?'

She answered cautiously. 'Mr Harrison, if this man was an obvious creep he'd never have impressed Jenny as he has. He's subtle, and clever.'

'You mean he's got to you?' Roscoe demanded.

'Certainly not!' she said quickly.

'Are you sure? Like you say, subtle and clever. Knows how to get any woman under his spell.'

'But I'm not any woman,' she told him crisply. 'I'm a woman who's seen through him before we started.

You can leave him to me. Tonight was stage one. Stage two will be my masterpiece.'

She hung up, feeling as though she'd been punched in the stomach. The call had brought her back to reality. What had she been thinking of to let this man weave fantasies about her when she knew the truth about him? It was simply—she searched for the worst word she knew—unprofessional.

But not any more, she assured herself. Tomorrow I'm going to be sensible.

Guido made his way through the streets by instinct and the fact that his feet knew the route by themselves. Lost in his blissful dream he didn't notice the two men approaching him until he collided with them.

'Apologies,' he murmured.

'Hey, it's us,' Marco said, grabbing his arm.

'So it is,' Guido agreed amiably.

'You weren't looking where you were going,' Leo accused him.

Guido considered. 'No, I don't think I was. Is this the way home?'

Any Venetian would have recognised this as an absurd question since, in that tiny city, all roads lead home. The other two looked at each other, then stationed themselves on either side of Guido like sentinels, and they finished the journey together.

The Palazzo Calvani had a garden that ran by the water. Marco signalled the butler to bring wine, and they all sat out under the stars.

'Don't talk, drink,' Marco ordered. 'There are few troubles that good wine can't cure.'

'I'm not in trouble,' Guido told him.

'What's got into you?' Marco demanded. 'Are you crazy?'

'I'm in love.'

'Ah!' Leo nodded wisely. 'That kind of crazy.'

'The perfect woman,' Guido said blissfully.

'What's her name?' Marco asked.

But Guido's sense of self-preservation was in good working order. 'Get lost,' he said amiably.

'When did you meet her?' Leo wanted to know.

'This afternoon. It happened in the first moment.'

'You always say they're after the title,' Leo reminded him.

'She doesn't know about the title, that's the best thing of all. She thinks I'm a gondolier, scratching a living, so I can be sure her smiles are for me. The one honest woman in the world.'

'Honest woman?' Marco echoed scathingly. 'That's asking a lot.'

'We're not all cynics like you,' Guido told him. 'Sometimes a man must trust his instincts, and my instincts tell me that she's everything that is good. Her heart is true, she's incapable of deception. When she loves me, it will be for myself alone.'

Leo raised his eyebrows. 'You mean she doesn't love you already? You're losing your touch.'

'She's thinking about it,' Guido insisted. 'She's going to love me—almost as much as I love her.'

'And you've known her how long?' Leo asked.

'A few hours and all my life.'

'Listen to yourself,' Marco snorted. 'You've taken leave of your senses.'

Guido held up a hand. 'Peace, you ignorant men!' he said sternly. 'You know nothing.'

He wandered away under the trees, leaving the other two regarding each other uneasily.

When he was out of their sight Guido stopped and looked up at the moon.

'At last,' he said ecstatically. 'She came to me. And she's perfect.'

CHAPTER FOUR

'I SHOULD be getting home soon,' Leo said next morning. 'I only came to see Uncle, and he's fine now.'

'Don't leave just yet,' Guido hastened to say. 'He sees you so seldom, and who knows how long he'll be around?'

They were having breakfast on the open-air terrace overlooking the water, relishing in the warm breeze and Liza's excellent coffee in equal measure.

'Uncle will outlive us all,' Leo insisted. 'I'm a farmer, and it's the busy time of year.'

'It's always the busy time of year, according to you.'

'Well, I don't like cities,' Leo growled. 'Hellish places!'

'Don't talk about Venice like that,' Guido said quickly.

'For pity's sake!' Leo said, exasperated. 'You're no more Venetian than I am.'

'I was born here.'

'We were both born here because Uncle made Poppa bring his wives to Venice for the births of their children. Same with Marco's mother. Calvani offspring must be born in the Palazzo Calvani.' Leo's tone showed what he thought of this idea. 'But we were both taken home to Tuscany when we were a few weeks old, and it's where we belong.'

'Not me,' Guido said. 'I've always loved Venice.'

As a child he'd been brought to stay with his uncle during school vacations, and when he was twelve

Francesco had made a complete takeover bid, demanding that he reside permanently in Venice so that he could grow up with the inheritance that would be his. Guido had only the vaguest idea about the inheritance but the city on the water entranced him, and he was glad of the move.

He had loved his father but was never entirely at ease with him. Bertrando was a countryman at heart, and he and Leo had formed a charmed duo from which Guido felt excluded. Bertrando had wept and wailed at the 'kidnap' of his son, but a large donation from Francesco to ease the effects of a bad harvest had reconciled him.

In due course Guido had come to feel his destiny as a poisoned chalice, but nothing could abate his love for the exquisite city. The fact that he'd made an independent fortune from catering to its tourists was, he would have said, an irrelevance.

Marco joined them a moment later, just finishing a call on his mobile phone. As he sat down he said, 'It's time I was going home.'

Guido went into overdrive. 'Not you as well. Uncle loves you being here. He's an old man and he doesn't see enough of you.'

'I'm neglecting business.'

'Banks run themselves,' Guido declared loftily.

This was flagrant provocation since he knew, and the others knew he knew, that Marco was far more than a simple banker. He was a deity of the higher finance, whose instinct for buying and selling had made many men rich and saved many others from disaster. Guido himself had profited by his advice to expand his business, but couldn't resist the chance to rib him now and then.

Marco bore up well under the treatment, ignoring

Guido's teasing, or perhaps he managed not to hear it.
Although his father had been a Calvani his mother was
Roman, and he lived in that city from choice. Austerely
handsome, proud, coolly aristocratic, unemotional and
loftily indifferent to all he considered beneath him, he
was Roman to his fingertips. Anyone meeting him for
a few minutes would have known that he came from
the city that had ruled an empire.

Just once he'd shown signs of living on the same
plane as other men. He'd fallen in love, become engaged and set the date for the wedding. His cousins had
been fascinated by the change in him, the warmth that
would flare from his eyes at the sight of his beloved.

And then it was all over. There was no explanation.
One day they were an acknowledged happy couple. The
next day the engagement was broken 'by mutual con-
sent'. The wedding was cancelled, the presents sent
back.

That had been four years ago, and to this day Marco's
sole comment had been, 'These things happen. We were
unsuited.'

'Unsuited?' Guido had echoed when Marco was
safely out of earshot. 'I saw his face soon after. Like a
dead man's. His heart was broken.'

'You'll never get him to admit it,' Leo had prophe-
sied wisely. And he'd been right.

Marco had never discussed the cancellation of his
wedding, and the others would have known nothing if
Guido hadn't happened to bump into the lady two years
later.

'He was too possessive,' she explained. 'He wanted
all of me.'

'Marco? Possessive?' Leo echoed when Guido related the conversation to him. 'But he's an iceberg.'

'Evidently not always,' Guido had observed.

It was doubtful if Marco would have confessed to the possession of a heart, broken or not. But these days he was never seen without a beautiful, elegant woman on his arm, although no relationship lasted for very long. In this respect his life might be said to resemble Guido's, but Guido's affairs sprang from the impetuous warmth of his nature, and Marco's from the calculating coolness of his.

He seated himself at the breakfast table now, ignoring Guido's attempts to rile him, and reached for the coffee. Instantly Lizabetta appeared with a fresh pot which she contrived to set down, remove the old one and clear away used dishes without speaking a word or appearing to notice their presence.

'She terrifies me,' Guido said when she'd gone. 'She reminds me of the women who knitted at the foot of the guillotine in the French revolution. When we're loaded into tumbrels and hauled off for execution Liza will be there, knitting the Calvani crest into a shroud.'

Leo grinned. 'They won't bother with me. I'm a hard-working son of the soil, and that's what I ought to be doing this minute.'

'Just a few more days,' Guido begged. 'It'll mean so much to Uncle.'

'To you, you mean,' Leo said. 'You just want us to occupy his attention while you get up to no good.'

'You're wrong,' Guido said, grinning. 'What I'm getting up to is very, very good.'

He was ahead of Dulcie getting to the landing stage, and for a horrid moment he was sure she wasn't coming. He knew he'd somehow put a foot wrong the previous night, but he could recover himself if he saw her again.

But she wasn't coming. She'd left the hotel, left Venice. He might never see her again…

There she was!

'Quickly,' he said, seizing her hand, 'the *vaporetto* is just coming.'

As the boat drew up he hurried her on board as though fearful that she might change her mind. He found her a seat at the side, near the prow, and sat silently, content to watch her as she beheld marvels unfold.

Dulcie could hardly believe that she was here. As she'd packed the black satin bikini she'd told herself that this was pointless because she wasn't really going to spend today with him. She'd stressed this again as she'd donned the scarlet sun dress, but then her feet had walked themselves out of the Empress Suite and into the lift.

And now here she was, sitting beside him as the *vaporetto* left the Grand Canal behind and settled in for the half-hour journey to the Lido, the strip of land that marked the boundary of the lagoon. The warm wind whistled past her, making her hair stream out, catching all her troubles and whirling them away across the blue water.

From the landing stage to the beach was just a short walk across the narrow island, and then she was gazing at an expanse of blue sea and golden sand that did her heart good.

He hired cubicles for them, and a huge umbrella which he ground into the sand. When she emerged from the cubicle wearing the bikini and a floating gauze top he'd already spread the towels on the sand and was waiting for her. His eyes never left her as she approached and slipped off the top, revealing a body that was slender, elegant and beautiful. She held her breath for his reaction.

'Where is your sun cream?' he demanded.

'My what?'

'With that fair skin you need it.'

'But I never catch the sun,' she protested.

'Nobody catches the sun in England because you don't have any. Not what I call sun. Here you need sun cream. Come, we'll go to the shop.'

Great, she thought, exasperated, as he steered her along the sand to the beach shop. That was all the reaction she was going to get.

In the shop he bought cream and a large straw hat. She protested until he settled the matter by ramming the hat onto her head, so that it covered her eyes and he had to lead her out, threatening dire retribution if she touched it. Only when they were back under the umbrella did he let her remove the hat and the top so that she could apply the cream.

'All over,' he instructed.

'Aren't you going to help me?'

'Sure. Turn around and I'll do your back and shoulders.'

He did exactly what he'd said without taking advantage. Her back and shoulders. Then he sat waiting while she covered every other inch of her. He didn't even offer to do her legs. Obviously, she thought, Jenny was very lucky and he was faithful to her.

So what were they doing here?

Perhaps he just wanted English female company, to remind him of the woman he really missed. It was a depressing thought. Except for Jenny, of course.

'Now we can have a swim,' he said, 'just a short one at first while you get used to the sun gradually.'

'It's like being taken out by my father,' she said indignantly.

'Was it really like this when he took you out?'

'No,' she admitted wryly. 'He never took me to the beach, it was always the races, and then he—well, he had other things to think about.'

'But didn't he ever just want to give you a treat?'

'No,' she said after a moment. There had been 'treats' for her brother, who'd been a chip off the old block, but, 'He said it was no fun taking me out because I didn't know how to enjoy myself.'

'Your father said *that*?' He sounded scandalised, and she had the same feeling as the night before, of having found her first sympathetic listener.

'He's just a big kid himself, really. He likes to have fun.'

'Well, today, *you* are going to have fun,' he declared. 'I am going to be the Poppa, and treat you to everything you want. We go swimming, we throw a beach ball, we eat ice lollies, we do everything.'

'Oh, yes,' she breathed. 'Yes, *please*.'

Grabbing her hand he began to race down the beach until they were in the shallows, where he danced about, splashing water onto her. She splashed back, thinking that nothing could have looked less like a 'Poppa'. He was lean and hard, with a smooth chest, a neat behind and long, muscular thighs.

Afterwards they strolled hand in hand along the edge of the water, for which he made her wear the sun hat again, although she felt no more than pleasantly warm in the brisk wind that swept along the shore. They stopped to rest by a little rock pool, and Dulcie let her toes dangle in the water, breathing in the salty air, and wondering how she'd lived without doing this.

'Watch out for crabs,' he said casually.

'*Aaargh*!' Her yell split the air as she snatched her toes away, while he laughed and laughed until she thought he would never stop. '*You rotten so and so—*' She was thumping him while he tried to fend her off, but not very effectively because he was weak from laughter. Somewhere in the tussle her hat vanished, whisked away by the wind and deposited out to sea.

'Are there really any crabs?' she asked, peering down into the water.

'Of course not, or I wouldn't have let you put your foot in there.'

'Well, you wait. I'll make you sorry, see if I don't,' she said, taking his hand for the return journey.

He led her to the beach restaurant and settled her at an outside table, under an awning, while he went inside, glancing hurriedly around. To his relief he saw only one person who knew his real identity. Nico was the son of one of the count's gardeners, earning extra in his college vacation. Guido grinned at him and murmured a few words in Venetian. Some notes changed hands.

After this, no more dodges, he promised himself as he walked out. *From now on I shall be as open and virtuous as she is herself. She has reformed me*.

The thought made him stop and consider. A reformed character.

A better man.

It'll be pipe and slippers next. You've always run a mile from them.

But who cares, as long as she's there?

He was grinning as he joined her at the table.

'What's so funny?' she asked.

'It's not funny exactly, it's just—have you ever suddenly looked around and found that life was a completely different shape to what you'd thought?'

'Well—'

But he didn't really want an answer. He was driven by the need to express the thoughts that overwhelmed him. 'Suddenly all the things you thought you'd never want became the objects of your desire—'

'How much did you drink while you were in there?'

'Why does everyone think I'm drunk? But I am!' he cried up to the sky. 'After all, there's drunk and drunk.'

'What are you talking about?' she chuckled.

'I don't know. I only know that—that—'

'Buon giorno, signore!'

It was Nico, being the perfect waiter. Guido ground his teeth. Surely there were other waiters? He gave the order and Nico departed, returning a moment later with pasta. He would have hovered further, enjoying the joke, but a look from Guido sent him scuttling off.

The food was delicious and Dulcie tucked in.

I shouldn't be enjoying this so much, she thought. *I'm here to work. But—just a few more hours, and then I'll be good.*

He was the perfect companion, telling her funny stories, refilling her glass with sparkling mineral water with as much of a flourish as if it were the finest wine. Afterwards he made her lie down in the shade for an hour before he would allow her to go into the sea.

But once in the water she was overcome with the longing to strike out. She was a strong swimmer and in a moment she was heading out to sea, ignoring his cry of protest, making him chase after her. By the time he caught up they were in deep water, and she was feeling good.

Laughing, she turned to face him, treading water, and found him wild-eyed.

'You crazy woman,' he said. 'To do such a thing in strange waters! You don't know what the currents are like.'

'You could always swim to my rescue,' she teased.

'And suppose I couldn't swim?'

'Oh, sure! A Venetian who can't swim! Even I know better than that!'

'I'm a lot feebler than I look,' he protested.

'Oh, yeah!'

'I've got a bad back,' he clowned. 'And a bad everything.'

'You look fine to me,' she said, surveying his smooth brown chest and muscular arms with pleasure.

'It's an illusion. Beneath this young exterior is the frame of a creaking old man, I swear it. In fact I— *Aaargh!*'

With a theatrical yell and a waving of arms he vanished beneath the water. Dulcie watched, amused, calculating when he would have to come up.

'Right,' she murmured. 'I said I'd get my own back. Watch this.'

She saw his shape reappearing below the surface from whatever depths he'd sunk to, and in the split second before his head broke the surface she slipped underwater, staying just close enough to hear his cry of, 'Dulcie! *Dulcie!* *Dio mio!* *Dulcie!*'

'Fooled you,' she said, coming up just behind him.

'You—*you*—!'

'Come on, it's only what you did to me.'

'You knew I was playing. I thought you'd drowned, you just vanished and—and—the whole ocean to search— *Come here!*'

'No way,' she said, seeing in his face that she'd pushed him just a little too far. Turning tail she began to swim back as fast as she could, managing to stay ahead, but only just. As soon as she reached the sand she began to run and covered several hundred yards before he caught up, seizing her arm.

'Ouch!' she said, for suddenly her skin stung where he touched it.

He released her at once. '*Basta*!' he said. Enough. 'You've been too long in the sun.'

He curved his arm near her shoulders, not touching, but insisting that she turn back to their umbrella. She found it was a relief. An ache was starting in the back of her head and she felt she'd had enough fun for one day.

'Sorry if I worried you,' she said.

'*Worried me*? Do you know—? No matter. I'll postpone my revenge.'

She lay down under the umbrella while he brought her a cold drink. It refreshed her a little, but the pleasure had gone out of the day, and when he suggested that they drift home she agreed. She was beginning to feel sleepy, and that made her annoyed with herself, because there was so much of the day left that she might have enjoyed.

On the journey back across the lagoon she stared out over the water, and must have dozed because suddenly it was time to disembark. Her nap hadn't made her feel any better, although she tried to seem brighter than she felt. The headache had now taken over completely. Her whole body felt hot and uncomfortable and the spell of the day was rapidly dissolving in a very prosaic feeling of being poorly.

'I've been thinking,' Guido began to say, but stopped as he looked at her. 'What's the matter with you?'

She tried to laugh. 'Just a bit of a headache.'

'Let me look at you.' He took gentle hold of her shoulders and turned her to face him. 'My poor girl!'

'What is it?' she asked, feeling more ill by the moment.

'Despite our precautions you've caught the sun badly. That fair skin of yours can't cope with this heat. I should have bought a stronger cream. Are you feeling bad?'

'Yes,' she said wretchedly. 'My head aches terribly.'

'Right, we're going home. Stay here.'

He settled her on a low stone wall and disappeared. She had no choice but to do as he'd said and stay there. The whole world seemed to be thundering inside her brain. She was only vaguely aware of him returning, saying, 'I've got us a taxi. Hold onto me.'

He half carried her down the steps to the boat, then sat in the back, holding her close, her head on his shoulder. She felt the vibration as the motor boat started up, the swift movement over the water, and the inexpressible comfort of his arms about her. The pain in her head was dreadful, yet she had a confused feeling that she could go on like this forever, if only he would hold her as he was doing now. Once she was vaguely aware of him making a call on his mobile phone, then everything went hazy again.

Then they were stopping and she was groping her way out, her eyes half closed, guided by him.

'Nearly there,' he said. 'You'll find the rest of the way more comfortable like this.' And he was lifting her in his arms.

She was too weak to protest, although she could

guess what a figure she must cut, being carried through the foyer of the Vittorio. How they would all be staring at her! She heard doors opening and closing behind them, then there was the blessed relief of being out of the sun.

'Thank you,' she murmured. 'What must they think of us?'

'Who?'

'The people in the hotel.'

'We're not in the hotel. I've brought you to my home.'

She managed to open her eyes and realised that she didn't recognise anything in her surroundings. Gone was the high, painted ceiling of the Empress Suite. There was no elaborate furniture or gilded decor, only a small, austerely furnished room, with wooden beams overhead. She was still in his arms and he was moving towards a door that he managed to pull open. With her eyes half closed she waited for him to lie her down. Instead she was set on her feet, and the next moment she was drenched in cold water.

She yelled with shock and made a feeble attempt to struggle, but he was holding her firmly to stop her falling.

'I'm sorry,' he yelled over the water, 'but getting under the shower is the quickest way to cool you off.'

'It's freezing,' she gasped.

'All the better. Lift your head. Let it pour over your face and neck. Please, you'll feel better.'

She did as he said. It felt good, insofar as anything could feel good at this moment. At last he turned the tap off and they stood there together, drenched and gasping.

'Here's the bath towel,' he said. 'I'll leave you alone

to get undressed.' But as he loosened his grip she nearly fell again. 'I'll have to do it for you,' he said.

'Will you?' she asked faintly.

He gritted his teeth. 'I'll force myself.'

He was very brave about it, loosening her buttons and slipping her dress off, then her sodden slip. Only her bra and panties were left.

'You've got to remove those too or you'll get pneumonia,' he said, working on them. At last she was naked, and he towelled her down until she was almost dry, then wrapped her in the vast towel like a parcel, and sat her on the stool while he ripped off his own soaking shirt.

'There's no point in me making you wet again,' he grunted, lifting her up.

This time he carried her into the bedroom and put her to bed, not unwrapping her until the last moment, then tucking the duvet up to her chin with his eyes averted.

'Don't worry about anything,' he said gently. 'It's quiet here and you can recover in peace.'

The next moment his front doorbell buzzed. When he returned he was accompanied by a plump middle-aged woman.

'This is Dr Valletti,' he explained. 'I called her on the way back. I want to be sure it isn't serious.'

He left the room at once. Dr Valletti regarded her with something akin to exasperation.

'You English! When will any of you learn to be sensible about the sun?'

'We don't have sunshine like this in England,' she said weakly. 'I did have a hat, but it blew away.'

'So I understand. And water magnifies the sun's rays. People with your fair colouring should stay covered up.'

She felt Dulcie's forehead, took her temperature and asked a few questions before pronouncing, 'You're lucky he got you under that cold shower fast. Now a day's rest in the cool will see off the worst. After that you take it easy for a while. You can go out, but only for a short time, and you cover up. Understand?'

'Yes, but I can't—'

'I'll leave these pills for your head. In summer I keep a supply on me, especially for the English. Goodbye now. Just do everything Gui—your friend tells you to. He's very worried.'

Through the throbbing in her head Dulcie heard only 'your friend' and 'very worried'. She lay back as the doctor departed, and vaguely sensed them talking behind the closed door. A few minutes later he entered the room, bearing a cup.

'Tea,' he announced, setting it down beside her. 'To take your pills. Let me help you up.'

His arm was firm beneath her back, raising her gently and holding her against his shoulder while she sipped the tea, which was perfectly made.

'You'll be nice and cool now, because I've turned the air-conditioning on,' he said as he laid her down again. 'When I've gone, try to get some sleep. Nobody will bother you, I promise.'

He went to the window and closed the shutters, making the room almost dark. Then he was gone. Dulcie lay still, willing the pills to take effect, and at last they began to do so. Gradually her consciousness slipped away.

She didn't know how much time had passed when she awoke. The light was dim because of the shutters. Her head was better but she still felt weak. His words, 'Nobody will bother you, I promise,' were there in her mind. He'd spoken them like a knight laying his sword on the bed between himself and his lady, a chivalrous vow of chastity.

It was a strange thought. This was the man she'd come here to expose as a liar and a cheap seducer. Yet he'd averted his eyes, as much as a man could avert his eyes from a woman he was undressing, and whatever her head might say, her heart instinctively trusted him.

She dozed, half awoke, dozed again, in the grip of a dream that seemed always to be with her, waking or sleeping. She was gliding, as if on an endless canal, but then suddenly she was falling endlessly. She reached out and felt her hand clasped by another which held her tightly, keeping her safe. With their fingers entwined she sensed all trouble fall away. Then she was gliding on again, and all about her was the sound of water and music, and happiness.

CHAPTER FIVE

SHE opened her eyes on total darkness. Her headache was gone and she felt light. Easing her way out of bed she discovered that she hadn't yet recovered. It took all her strength to walk to the window and undo the shutters.

Outside was a world of calm shadows. It was dark, the only light coming from the moon seeking to penetrate the narrow canals below. This little apartment seemed to be in a backwater, with a narrow canal, or *rio* running beneath. She couldn't tell where she was, except that this wasn't the glamorous part of the city. It was the homely part, where the Venetians lived. A young couple wandered along the opposite bank, dressed almost alike in jeans and sweaters. They looked up, saw her watching them and vanished into the shadows.

Switching on the bedside light she saw that the bathrobe was now lying on the bed, although it hadn't been there when she'd fallen asleep. When had he done that? She had no idea, but there was no doubt he'd entered the room and left it without disturbing her.

She realised that she was still more overheated than she'd thought, because the fire that had consumed her body earlier hadn't quite died down. Either that or it was the knowledge that he'd looked at her while she was oblivious.

She slipped the cotton robe on and quietly opened the bedroom door. It led straight into a large living room, also in darkness except for moonlight. By its light she managed to identify the bathroom, and crept in, closing the door silently behind her.

The first thing she saw was her sodden clothes hanging over the bath, perfectly arranged, as if by an artist.

The sight of herself in the mirror was a shock. Her normal pale colour had given way to a pink that she didn't find becoming. Under the bathrobe her shoulders felt tender, and a glimpse beneath it showed her the worst. The sun had burned her wherever it had touched.

'So much for the temptress,' she thought wryly. 'Turning into a lobster wasn't part of the plan.'

She splashed cold water on her face, but it didn't do much for her. She'd used up a lot of strength just getting this far, and the journey back looked like a marathon.

Emerging from the bathroom she had a clear view of someone sleeping on the sofa. Since he was a tall man and it was a short sofa his discomfort was evident, even under the duvet that half covered him. Her face softened as she viewed him, wondering how long he'd been there, and what state he would be in when he awoke.

She began to make her way back to the bedroom, but it was hard because her remaining strength was seeping away fast. After a few steps she stopped, clinging onto a chair, breathing hard, her forehead damp. The next chair was three feet away. She began to plan how she would make it, short steps, sliding her feet along an inch at a time, then a quick dash.

She managed the first bit all right, but she miscalculated the dash, fell short by several inches and collided hard with the sofa, making its occupant slide to the floor and awaken, tangled in the duvet and cursing vividly.

'I'm sorry,' she gasped, clinging onto the back of the sofa.

He was on his feet in a moment, a lithe, smooth-chested figure in shorts and nothing else. 'It's all right,' he said quickly. 'Here. Hold onto me.'

She did so, thankfully. 'I thought I was better,' she murmured, 'but when I got up—I just don't know—'

'You don't get over this sort of thing in five minutes. It'll take a day or two. How's your headache?'

'It had gone, but it's coming back.'

'Let's get you into bed then, and I'll make you some tea and you can have two more of those pills. The doctor left me complete instructions.'

They had reached the bed but he put her into a chair and held up a finger to tell her to stay there. Then he descended on the bed in a whirl of activity, finding fresh pillowcases, smoothing the undersheet and shaking the duvet out until it was fluffy.

'You're very domesticated,' she said admiringly.

'My father taught me. He said you should never depend on women for these things because they weren't reliable.' He spoke with a straight face, but his eyes twinkled. 'Back to bed.'

She made a move as if to undo the robe, but then remembered that she had nothing on underneath. He pointed to some drawers. 'You'll find some vests in there.' He left.

She chose one of his vests and had slipped back into bed by the time he returned with tea. She drank it thankfully and took more pills for the headache which had returned with a vengeance.

'There's a little bell by the bed,' he said, removing the cup and settling her. 'Ring it if you need me.'

'You're a wonderful nurse,' she murmured, sliding down contentedly.

'Go to sleep.'

This time she slept long and awoke feeling refreshed. Throwing open the shutters she found a brilliant morning and took some long, deep breaths. Her head was better, although she still felt wobbly.

Donning the robe, she peered around the bedroom door, but found no sign of her host. In a small, single-floor apartment, with all rooms leading off the main one, it took no time to ascertain that he'd gone out.

It was a peaceful, pleasant place, with white walls, a cool terrazzo floor, and furniture that was sparse and functional. The only sign of flamboyance was the profusion of masks that hung on the walls. Some were simple, some fantastic with long noses and sinister slits for the eyes. They seemed to cover every wall, and Dulcie surveyed them with interest.

Looking at the tiny sofa she winced with sympathy for him. It seemed so unfair for him to sleep in that cramped place while she had his whole double bed at her disposal.

But of one thing there was no further possible doubt. This was a man who had very little money.

An inspection of her dress in the bathroom showed that it was unwearable after its drenching. An inspection of herself showed that the pink of her skin had faded, but still wasn't a colour she'd have chosen. She was considering how matters stood when she heard the front door open, and went out to see him enter, loaded down with shopping. She hastened to rescue some bags that were slipping from his fingers.

'Dump them in the kitchen,' he said. 'No, just these. I'll take those.' He whisked a couple of items away from her, dropped them on the sofa and guided her into the kitchen. 'You're looking better.'

'I feel it. I just wish I looked it.'

'Good healthy colour.'

'T'isn't! It just tells the world I'm an idiot.'

'I'm not answering that. Let me sit down. I've been staggering under this lot for too long.'

'Shall I make you some coffee?'

'No thank you,' he said with more speed than gallantry.

'Why not?'

'Because you're English,' he said, not mincing matters.

'Meaning we don't know how to make coffee?'

He just grinned and rose to his feet. 'I'll make the coffee for both of us, then I'll get your breakfast. Something light I think. Soup, and then—yes, that would be it.'

He refused to say any more, watching her with a glint of mischief as she helped him unpack the food. He seemed to have shopped for an army.

'I've been having a look at my dress,' she said.

'Did the shower leave it in a state? Sorry about that. I suppose I should have ripped it off you first.'

'No, you shouldn't,' she said firmly. 'I'm not complaining, you did the right thing. It's just that I'm having visions of me going back to the Vittorio looking a fright.'

'You don't have to do that. Go and have a look at the bags in the other room.'

Puzzled, she did so, and her eyes widened at the contents.

'I knew you'd be needing some fresh clothes,' he said, standing in the kitchen doorway and watching her.

'It's just cheap stuff from market stalls, and not what you're used to.'

That made her feel bad because it was exactly what she was used to. He'd bought her a pair of white jeans and two coloured tops to go with them. And he'd assessed her size perfectly, as she realised when she considered the other items.

'You had the cheek to buy me—?'

'You need underwear,' he said defensively. 'Excuse me, the coffee's perking.'

He vanished into the kitchen and closed the door, leaving Dulcie examining the bras and panties that he'd chosen for her. They were lacy, delicate confections, designed to be seen. A woman would choose such things if she planned to undress in front of a man. And a man would choose them if he wanted to see them on a woman, or wanted to see the woman remove them, or wanted to think about her wearing and/or removing them.

Dulcie hastily silenced her thoughts. But what she couldn't shut out was the way he'd hurried away and put a door between them. It was almost as though he was shy as well as shameless.

Further investigation revealed a nightgown. Unlike the underwear it was fiercely sexless, unadorned cotton, with a front that buttoned up to the neck. She sat for a while, contemplating the prosaic nightgown on the one hand and the sexy underwear on the other. There was no understanding him. Which was strange, considering how simple she'd expected him to be.

She glanced up as the kitchen door opened again, and one eye appeared. It looked nervous.

'Oh, come on,' she said, chuckling.

The other eye appeared. 'The coffee's ready. Am I forgiven?'

'I'm not sure,' she said, joining him in the kitchen, where he set coffee before her. 'You had a cheek buying me panties that look like that.'

'But I like them,' he said innocently.

'And you had an even bigger cheek buying me a nightie that my grandmother could wear.'

His hint of mischief disappeared. 'I think I was right,' he said simply. 'While you are ill it's better that you look...' he hesitated '...like a grandmother. At least, not a grandmother exactly because you could never look like that but—safe. You must feel safe.' He tore his hair. 'I'm not saying this very well—but perhaps you understand—'

'Yes,' she said, touched. 'I do understand you. It's very kind of you to think of my safety.'

'Somebody has to think of it. You're shut up here alone with a man of bad character, enfeebled by illness, nobody to protect you if you shout for help.'

'Perhaps he isn't a man of bad character.'

'But he is. Definitely. You should dress in sensible clothes to prevent him indulging in disgraceful thoughts about—' he caught her enquiring eyes on him '—about what you would look like if you weren't wearing sensible clothes, or even if you weren't wearing—I'll start the soup,' he finished hurriedly.

Dulcie's lips twitched. She wasn't fooled by this apparent boyish confusion, but she appreciated the way he'd paid her a compliment without getting heavy about it.

'But I shan't be here long,' she said. 'I can go back to the hotel when I've eaten.'

'I don't think so. You're not well yet, and the doctor

is coming for you again today. You feel strong now, but it won't last.'

In fact her strength was already fading, and when he set soup before her she took it gladly. This was followed by a bowl of rice and peas, cooked to perfection. A few more hours' rest would set her up, she told herself as she headed back to bed, to find that it had been freshly made. She slipped on the 'grannie' nightgown and got thankfully back under the duvet.

This time, when she awoke, it was to find Dr Valletti just entering the room.

'Yes, you seem better,' she agreed when she'd checked Dulcie over. 'But take it easy for another day. Tomorrow you can go out, but only for short periods, and keep covered up against the sun.'

'I'm really well enough to go back to the hotel,' she said guiltily when the doctor had departed.

'No,' he said at once. 'You must stay here where I can look after you. In the hotel there are only servants. What do they care for you?'

She made a face. 'If I tip them well enough, they'll care.'

'Oh, yes. Is that kind of caring enough?'

She shook her head.

'Besides,' he added, 'I don't trust you.'

'I beg your pardon!'

'You'll do something stupid if I'm not there. So you stay here where I can watch over you. And I don't want a tip.'

'Well, maybe I'll leave it for now. I'll go tomorrow.'

'You'll go when I say.'

'Yes *sir*! Is it all right if I get up now and take a shower?'

While he cooked supper she showered and donned

some of the lacy underwear, thinking it was a pity that her complexion wasn't more becoming. She selected the pale-yellow top to go with the white jeans. Now her appearance was simple and elegant, and much more to her own taste than the elaborate confections she had hanging up in the hotel.

'What are you cooking?' she asked, sauntering into the kitchen and standing where he could see her.

'To start with, mushroom risotto.' He paused from chopping parsley and stood back to regard her. '*Bene!* Very nice!'

'You think so?'

'Yes, I got the size exactly right. I was wondering about that. Can you hand me that onion?'

She nearly threw it at him.

At his instruction she laid the little table for two by the open window. It was evening and a soft, bluey light lay over the scene outside. Lamps were coming on, reflected in the water, and from somewhere in the distance came the echoing warnings of the gondoliers, sounding like melancholy music.

He opened a bottle of *prosecco*, a sparkling white wine.

'It's very light,' he explained, 'so it won't upset your stomach.'

They chinked glasses.

'In fact, I've arranged the whole meal to be light,' he explained. 'The next course is pasta and beans, then a shrimp omelette. And to finish—fried cream.'

'Fried—? You're kidding me.'

'No, I promise. You shall watch.'

And she did watch as he blended flour, sugar, eggs and milk into a thick cream, that he proceeded to fry. It was delicious.

Afterwards he washed while she dried, wondering at a certain embarrassment in his manner.

'Is something the matter?' she asked.

'Well—Dulcie would you mind if—when we've finished this?—only if you want to, of course—'

'What is it?' she asked with a little pang of dismay. Here it came, the amorous advance that would make him cheap in her eyes. It was what she'd come here for, and suddenly she would have given anything to put him off.

But duty came first, so she merely looked at him expectantly while her heart beat with apprehension.

He took a deep breath and went on with the air of a man plunging off the deep end. 'There's a really important soccer match on television tonight—'

'A soccer match?'

'It's Juventus playing Lazio, or I wouldn't ask,' he pleaded. 'You don't mind?'

'No,' she said, dazed. 'I don't mind.'

They spent the rest of the evening sitting side by side on the sofa, holding hands, until he declared that it was time for her to go to bed. But he had to say it twice because she'd fallen asleep against his shoulder.

Next morning he let her sleep late, and she awoke knowing that the last of her illness had gone. While dressing she noticed with delight that she was no longer red. The colour had softened into a light tan that looked marvellous against her fair hair and green eyes, and even better against the soft-pink top that she matched with the white jeans.

'Who won the match?' she asked, appearing in the kitchen.

'I forget. You look great. How do you feel?'

It was on the tip of her tongue to say she felt splendid, but she amended it to, 'Better than I did, but not quite my normal self.'

That was true, she told her conscience. She would never feel like her normal self again.

'Then we'll take it easy today. A light breakfast, then a gentle walk.'

His solicitude made Dulcie feel a little guilty because she'd allowed him to think her more frail than she actually was. But, to someone who'd lived such a practical life, there was a sweet pleasure in being cosseted, and she reminded herself that her mission was to discover the truth about him. If the truth turned out to be that he was a marvellous man, kind, gentle, affectionate, considerate and chivalrous, then she would report this truth and be happy for Jenny.

Over rolls and coffee he said, 'I have to buy food this morning, so we can take a stroll.'

'You mean I've eaten you out of house and home?'

'You've hardly touched anything.'

She was about to mention the clothes he'd bought her, then hesitated, remembering the first night, the intensity in his voice as he'd said, 'Please don't insult me with money.'

Suddenly inspired she said, 'Let me cook something for you today. An English meal.'

He regarded her quizzically. 'Her Ladyship can cook?'

'Her Ladyship spent lots of time with the cook because she was the most interesting person in the house,' Dulcie said truthfully. 'And the kindest. She was almost a mother to me after my own died. And she made me learn everything she knew. She thought it might come in handy one day.'

'You mean when the revolution happened and the tumbrels came for you?' he teased.

'Well—' she considered, also teasing '—if I was being carried off to the guillotine I'm not sure that cooking would help me much, but you've got the general idea. I'm sure Sarah pictured little old ladies sitting at the foot of the guillotine, knitting the Maddox family crest into a shroud. What's the matter?' she asked quickly, for he'd dropped a dish on the floor, where it shattered.

'Nothing,' he said hastily, dropping down to clear the pieces.

'You jumped. Was it something I said?'

'Just a feeling of having been here before. Let's go out and get food.'

He took her to the market by the Rialto Bridge where the food stalls stretched in profusion, and he pointed out fruit, vegetables, meat and fish. But he kept himself at a slight distance, and then slid out of sight while she did the buying, which puzzled her even while she appreciated that it gave her the chance to pay for the food without upsetting him.

Afterwards he took the bags from her, refusing to let her carry even one, and they strolled hand in hand.

'This isn't the way we came,' she said, looking around. 'At least, I don't think so, but the streets all look the same.'

'No, we're going a different way. I thought we'd take a detour through St Mark's Square. You haven't seen it yet.'

In St Mark's he took her to an outside table at one of the many cafés and they sat drinking coffee and listening to the music from a four-piece orchestra. Dulcie crumbled up a small cake and fed it to some of the thousands of pigeons that thronged the visitors. The sun hadn't reached its height, making it no more than pleasantly warm, and she leaned back, eyes closed, over-whelmed by a blissful content that she could never remember feeling before.

She opened her eyes at last, turning to him, smiling, and caught an unguarded expression on his face. His feelings were there, open and defenceless. It was a look not merely of love but almost of adoration, with nothing held back, and it took her breath away. Beneath his smiles and jokes there was *this*?

Then a sound disturbed the pigeons and they rose up with a wild beating of wings, thousands of them, darkening the sky, making the air swirl. Her head spun, though whether it was the pigeons or what she had just seen Dulcie was too confused to know.

And when the flight was over and she could see him again she found that he was rising, gathering bags and saying things about leaving. She managed to take a bag in the teeth of his protests, and they wandered away along the waterfront until it was time to turn inland where some of the *calles* were so narrow that she had to walk behind him, but still with her hand clasped in his.

In her mind she could still see his face, transported with joy yet with a strange look of peace, like a man who'd come home and found it a blissful place. She wanted to close her eyes against that look, and she wanted to see it all her life.

'What is it?' he asked, looking back at her. 'You're lagging behind. Are you tired?'

'No, I'm fine.'

'I've kept you out too long.' He slipped an arm about her shoulders. The smile he gave her was almost like those she'd seen before, just friendly. But behind it she could see the shadow of the other look. She slipped an arm about his waist and let him guide her home through streets of gold.

CHAPTER SIX

HE ORDERED her to rest in front of the television while he unpacked the food in his tiny kitchen, and made her a cup of tea. Remembering his strictures about English coffee she was half looking forward to returning the compliment, but the tea was excellent.

She spent the afternoon at work in the kitchen while he helped with the 'menial tasks', fetched and carried and generally did as he was told, but with an air of meekness that belied the wicked glint in his eyes.

Several times she glanced at him, wondering if she would catch the intense look that had seemed to suggest so much, but he had himself under command now. Except that often she sensed him watching her too.

But he had his timetable, she knew that now. While she was officially an invalid he would act like her brother. And after that she would be gone, she remembered with a little ache.

In the early evening they sat down to eat and her meal was a triumph. He approached it cautiously, as if to say that he'd heard about English cooking but was prepared to be kind. He ended up scraping the plate and asking for more.

Afterwards he settled her on the sofa with a glass of *prosecco*, while he prepared the coffee. When he returned she was reclining peacefully on the sofa, admiring the masks on his wall.

'Ah, you're looking at my *zanni*,' he said, setting the cups on a low table.

'*Zanni*?'

'It means clowns. In English you would say they are "zany". Most of the masks there are clowns, Harlequin, Columbine, Pierrot, Pierrette, but there are others too because masks have always been so important in Venice, right back to the thirteenth century. Ladies of the night would offer themselves in a variety of "faces", aristocrats who wanted to indulge themselves anonymously. And sometimes the "ladies of pleasure" and the "great ladies" were the same. There were couples who grew very amorous—then removed the masks and discovered they'd been married for years.'

'All very disreputable,' she said.

'A lot of it was, which was why at different times in Venice's history masks have been banned. They concealed a little too much.'

'You make it sound as though masks were Venice's exclusive preserve, but surely every civilisation has appreciated them.'

He shrugged. 'Certainly, you'll find them in other countries, but it was the Venetians who turned them into an art form.'

'But why? Why you and not the others?' she asked, genuinely interested.

'Perhaps it's something to do with the Venetian character, a certain fluidity.'

'What exactly do you mean, fluidity?'

He grinned. 'Unkind people have called it unscrupulous. We are not a solid, respectable race. How can we be?' He indicated the canal beneath the window. 'We don't live on solid foundations. We travel through streets that move beneath us. Our city is sinking into the lagoon, and it has changed hands so often through the centuries that life itself isn't solid. We live on our wits, and we've learned a certain—let's say—adaptability. And the best way to be adaptable, is to keep a variety of masks available.'

'A variety?'

'One is never enough. Over the centuries we've played so many roles. We've conquered the surrounding areas, and in our turn we've been conquered. Venetians have been both masters and servants, and we know that each is just a role to be played, with its proper mask. Come and look more closely.'

She did so, wondering at the variety of expressions that could be encompassed by a little painted cardboard.

'There are so many. It's incredible.'

'There are as many as there are expressions on the human face, or types of the human heart.'

'Then how is anyone to know who you really are?'

'Because sooner or later each person dons the mask that reveals the truth.'

'But which truth?' she asked quickly, 'when the truth itself is always shifting?'

He made a sudden alert movement. 'You understand. Something told me that you would. Of course, you're right. I can only say that when people's faces are hidden they are free to become their true selves.'

'Then their selves shift also, and they become another self,' she pressed him. It was somehow important.

'Of course they do,' he countered. 'Because people turn into different people all the time. Are you the same person you were last year, last week, the day before you came to Venice?'

'No,' she said slowly. 'Not at all.'

He took down a mask with a very long nose and held it before his face. 'Pantalone, the merchant, greedy for profit.' He changed the mask for one with a shorter nose, but ugly. 'Pulcinella, he's a bit of a thug. In England you call him Mr Punch.' Another change to a broad, plump mask. 'The doctor, spouts yards of pseudo science.'

He whisked another mask off the wall and held it up so that his eyes looked through the slits. It was uncannily like his own face.

'Harlequin,' he said. 'His name derives from Hellecchino, which means "little devil". He's like a rubber ball, always bouncing back: cunning and inventive, but not as clever as he thinks he is, and his mistakes always bring him to the edge of disaster. He wears a multi-coloured costume because his kind friends have given him their old cast-offs to sew together.'

'Poor fellow,' she said laughing. 'And are you like him?'

'What makes you say that?' he asked quickly.

'You say more about him than the others.'

'True. Yes, I suppose I do. I hadn't realised. But that's my point. A man may be Harlequin today and Pantalone tomorrow.'

'You, the greedy merchant?'

'Well, a merchant anyway.' Almost to himself, he added, 'With a pipe and slippers.'

He saw her puzzled look and hastened to change the subject. 'Anyway, it's good to see you laugh. You don't laugh enough.'

'I laugh a lot with you.'

'But not at other times. I wonder why.'

'You don't know what I'm like at other times.'

'I think I do. Something tells me that you're a too-serious person.' He touched her arm lightly. 'You let yourself get burned because you're not used to spending

time in the sun. That's not just true of your body. Your
mind and spirit aren't used to the sunshine.'

She was about to tell him that this was nonsense,
when she was overwhelmed by the sense of its truth.
Watching her, he saw the dawning of comprehension in
her face.

'Why?' he said. 'It's not just because of the man who
broke your heart.'

'No, it's not,' she said slowly.

Her mind was ranging back over a sea of memories.
How old had she been when she'd sensed that her family lived on a knife-edge? When had she started doing
the sums for her father? He'd never been able to add,
perhaps because the truth was too frightening to know.

She'd been fifteen when she'd cried— 'Dad, you
can't afford it. You're in so much debt already.'

'Then a little more can't hurt, can it? C'mon sweetie,
don't pull a long face.'

A charmer, her father. But a selfish charmer who'd
taught her the meaning of fear without ever knowing it.
She'd built her own defences, working hard at school,
promising herself a brilliant career. But it hadn't happened. She'd ended up without a single exam pass, because a run of ill luck had convinced her father of the
need for a long stay abroad. When they returned a year
later her chance had passed. So she'd found a job where
she could live on her wits, because in the end, they were
all she had.

'Tell me,' he begged, his eyes on her face.

'No,' she said quickly. This tale of poverty wasn't
for him. 'You're right, I've been too serious.'

'Maybe it's time to put on another mask. Perhaps you

should be Columbine. She's a sensible person, but she's also sharp and witty, and can see life's funny side.'

'Which one is she?'

The mask he took down was painted silver, adorned with sequins and tiny coloured feathers. He fitted it gently over her face and tied the satin ribbons behind.

'What do you think?' she asked, regarding herself in the mirror. Almost all her face was covered, with only her mouth showing.

To her surprise he shook his head. 'No, I don't think so.'

'Why? I like it. Shall I try another?'

'No. Somehow I don't think masks are right for you. Not you. Well, not this one. She's charming, but she's also a deceiver, and you could never be that. Look at the sequins, how they flash and catch a different light every time. That's Columbine, but it's not you.'

She looked at him, wondering if she'd understood his meaning, and feeling uneasy.

The telephone shrilled.

It took her a moment to realise that it was her own mobile phone, ringing from her bag on the floor. She'd been too poorly to think of switching it off. Frantically she dived for it.

'Why haven't you called me?' Roscoe's voice rasped.

'It's been difficult the last few days,' she said in a low, hurried voice. 'I can't talk now.'

'Why not? Are you with him?'

'Yes.'

'Going great then?'

'Yes. Fine. Wonderful. I'll call you later. Goodbye.'

She hung up and switched the phone off. Her heart was beating hard. Roscoe was a terrible intrusion from the outside world, one she would have given anything to avoid. But it was too late now.

'Is everything all right?' he asked.

'Of course. Everything's fine,' she said brightly.

But it wasn't. Nothing was fine.

She realised that she was still wearing the mask and hastily pulled it off.

'Must you really go so soon?' he begged her the next morning. 'Stay another day.'

'No,' Dulcie said hurriedly. 'I can't take up any more of your time. After all, that gondola is your living, and you've already lost several days' work because of me.'

He hesitated, then plunged on. 'Actually, I don't rely on the gondola to live. There's something about myself I have to tell you—'

Suddenly she was filled with dread. It was coming, the pretence of being a Calvani. And only now did she understand how much she'd relied on him not making any such claims. Without that she could still see him as an honest man, and if she lost that belief it would hurt almost as much as saying goodbye to him.

'Dulcie—'

'Not now,' she said quickly. 'I have to get back. I have things to do—' She knew she wasn't making sense but she was desperate to stop him.

'You're right,' he said. 'This isn't the moment. Will you meet me tonight?'

'All right.'

He went down to the water with her and hailed a motor taxi. She kept her eyes on him as it drew away, feeling heavy hearted. Whatever happened tonight the magic that had encompassed her for the last few days was over. If he started spinning tales about being a

Calvani he would confirm her worst fears. If not, he was an honest man, and belonged to Jenny.

Casting her mind back over the last few days she was unable to recall anything that could be read as the behaviour of a lover. Even that searing moment in the square might have been her imagination, although her heart told her it wasn't. Apart from that there had been the odd semi-flirtatious remark. If she hadn't become ill and dumped herself on him, it would all have been over after the day on the beach.

And if her own heart had somehow become entangled she could only blame herself for being unprofessional, and sort it out as best she could. Alone. Away from here. One way or another, tonight would mark the end.

As she entered the Empress Suite her phone was already ringing.

'It took me time enough to get through to you,' Roscoe grumbled.

'I'm sorry, Mr Harrison, I've been very occupied.'

'With this Fede character?'

'Yes.'

'Has he given you his Calvani story?'

'Not exactly—'

'Aha! You mean he's laying the ground. That's how he dazzled Jenny. Now, you check that out. This Calvani character must have an heir. Find him. See what he looks like. Call me back when you've done that.'

He hung up.

Dulcie glared at the dead phone, at the world in general. 'So how am I going to—'

And then she heard a voice speaking far off in her memory.

'Such a handsome man, my dear. We were all madly in love with him, and he loved all of us.'

Lady Harriet Maddox, her grandfather's sister, and a dazzling beauty in her day. She'd scorched her way around Europe, flirting outrageously and leaving a trail of broken hearts, before marrying a man with no title but a large bank balance, which she'd proceeded to gamble away.

She was always discreet about her indiscreet past, but there was one man whose memory could bring a warm light to her eyes—if only Dulcie could recall his name. Harriet had travelled in Italy and probably met Count Calvani among many others, but was he the one she'd called 'the latter-day Casanova'?

'He could have been,' Dulcie mused, 'And that's all I need. Right. To work.'

It took three hours to get her appearance exactly right, but when she left the hotel she was satisfied. Her attire was costly and elegant without being over-the-top, and she looked every inch *Lady* Dulcie.

A water taxi took her to the Palazzo Calvani, and a steward came to meet her.

'Is Count Calvani at home?' she asked.

'I am not quite sure, *signorina*,' the man replied. 'If I could have your name—?'

'I am Lady—' she stopped, suddenly swept by the wild gambling instinct that bedevilled her family '—please tell him that Lady Harriet Maddox is here.'

He bowed and retired, leaving Dulcie wondering if she'd gone quite mad.

She didn't have to wait long to find out. There was a hasty step on the marble floor, a voice calling, '*Carissima*,' and she turned to see an elderly man standing there, his look of pleasure dissolving into bafflement. Even through his lines and white hair she could see the remains of remarkable good looks.

'Forgive me,' she said quickly, advancing with her hands outstretched. 'I gave you the name of my great-aunt in the hope that you would remember it as well as she remembered you.'

He stretched out his own hands and clasped hers warmly. '*Bellisima Harriet*,' he said. 'How well I remember her! And how kind of you to visit me.'

He kissed her on both cheeks and looked warmly into her eyes. Although he must have been at least seventy, his charm was still dazzling and Dulcie felt its full effect. But she was unable to detect the slightest resemblance to the man with whom she'd spent the last few days.

'So you are not Lady Harriet?' he asked. 'You are—?''

'I am Lady Dulcie.'

The count commanded refreshment to be served on the terrace, and led her out there with her hand tucked in his arm, and his own other hand holding it. He handed her to a seat with an air of old-world gallantry, only releasing her hand at the very last moment.

'I'm an old man,' he said sadly, 'and it's so rare for me to have the pleasure of a beautiful woman on my arm. You'll forgive me if I make the most of it?'

He was a shameless fraud, she thought, entertained by his slightly theatrical air. But it was easy to imagine him as 'the latter-day Casanova'.

Over coffee and cakes he demanded to know all about her family in England.

'Dear Harriet told me about Maddox Court where she grew up,' he recalled, 'and about her brother William—'

'My grandfather.'

'Still alive I hope?'

'No, he died fifteen years ago.'

'Then it is your father who is now the earl?'

'Yes. But tell me about your family, your wife and children.'

'Alas,' he said mournfully, 'I'm just a lonely old bachelor, with no wife or children to comfort my old age.'

And I'm the Queen of the May, she thought, amused. *You're just like my Uncle Joe who was fighting paternity suits in his sixties.*

Aloud she said, 'You mean you live in this great place, all alone?'

'Well, there are servants,' he said with a sigh. 'But what are servants when a man is lonely? I have a nephew who will one day be the count. He's a good boy, but not a comfort to me as a son would be.'

'A nephew?' she echoed, speaking lightly as though this was a matter of total indifference to her.

'Three actually. The other two live in different parts of the country, but they're visiting me now, and I should so like it if you would come to dinner with us this evening, and meet all three of them.'

'That would be lovely.'

'And please bring whoever is in Venice with you. Your husband perhaps?'

'I have no husband, and I'm here alone.'

'You must seek a husband in Venice,' he said at once. 'We make the best husbands.'

'But how do you know?' she teased him, 'if you've never tried being one.'

He laughed heartily. '*Bravissima*. A lady of wit. Now I look forward to this evening even more. My boat will call for you at eight o'clock.' He rose and took her hand again, leading her out to the landing stage where the gleaming white Calvani boat was waiting to take her back to the hotel.

He stood watching until the boat was out of sight. Then he returned to the terrace to finish the wine. Leo and Marco found him there, looking pleased with himself.

'What mischief are you up to?' Leo demanded at once.

'Merely protecting my family line,' Francesco said with relish. 'I've introduced suitable women to Guido until I've grown exhausted doing it. But never let it be said I've shirked my duty. I thought there was nobody else left, but she'll do very well.'

'She? Who?' they both wanted to know.

'A lady of birth and breeding, and moreover, related to an old flame of my own.'

Leo began to protest, 'But half the women in Europe are related to your—'

'Silence. Show some respect. She's coming to dinner tonight, and he'll meet her.'

'But he won't be here,' Marco observed. 'He called to say he won't be home tonight.'

'Whatever engagement he has, he will break it.'

'Uncle, there's something you should—'

'Enough. I expect you all to present yourself for dinner, properly attired out of respect for our guest. Now I shall take a nap, as I wish to be at my best tonight.'

Never had paperwork seemed more boring than the mountain of it that confronted Guido when he returned to work after playing hookey to be with Dulcie. He ploughed through it grimly, comforting himself with the thought of the evening ahead, when he would see her again.

He would take her out to a restaurant a safe distance from Venice where he could pass unrecognised, although soon that would cease to matter, because he would tell her the truth about himself.

He wondered if she would blame him for his innocent deception. Surely not, when once he'd poured out his heart to her? While she was ill and dependent on him he'd restrained himself, carefully editing out all passion, and even love. He could recall a few moments when his resolution had frayed, but he'd pulled himself back into line. No words had been spoken, but he knew they had understood each other perfectly. She *must* love him as he loved her. It was impossible that he should be mistaken about her.

Lost in his happy dream he didn't at first hear the ring of his mobile phone and had to snatch it up hastily.

'Where the devil are you?' his uncle barked.

'In my office, working hard,' Guido said with a conscious attempt to sound virtuous.

It was wasted. 'You've got time for all those knick-knacks you call a business, and time to fool around, but no time for your old uncle.'

'That's not fair—'

'I've hardly seen you this last week.'

'You've had Leo and Marco, you didn't need me.'

'Well, I need you tonight. We're having a dinner party for a very special guest.'

'Uncle please, not tonight, I've made plans—'

'Nonsense, of course you haven't. It's all arranged. A beautiful lady is coming to dinner, and she's looking forward to meeting you.'

Guido groaned. Another prospective wife. Would his uncle never learn? And how could he sit through this evening knowing that his heart had already chosen his future wife.

'Uncle, let me explain—'

Francesco's voice grew mournful. 'There's no need to explain. I'm an old man and I ask for very little. If even that little is too much, well, I suppose I understand.'

Guido ground his teeth as he always did when Francesco went into 'forlorn mode', because he knew he was going to give in. He was fond of his uncle and couldn't bear to hurt him. His blissful evening began to recede.

'All right, I'll try to make it,' he said.

'You're a good boy. I don't want to be a trouble. Of course when a man gets to my age he always *is* a trouble—'

'Uncle will you cut it out?' Guido yelled. 'I'll be there, I swear it.'

'All evening?'

'All evening.'

'In a dinner jacket?'

'In a dinner jacket.'

'I knew you wouldn't let me down. Don't be late.' He hung up.

Guido drew a long breath. Why did life have to be so complicated? And how was he going to explain to Dulcie that he was standing her up to meet a woman his uncle wanted him to marry. No, he hastily decided against that. Whatever excuse he found, the truth was out of the question. Another mask, he thought despondently. Never mind. Soon all that would be over.

CHAPTER SEVEN

THE evening dress Dulcie chose was a stunning, ice-blue floral Jacquard that left her arms and shoulders bare. Dainty diamond studs winked in her ears and a diamond pendant hung about her throat. Now that she'd become an attractive pale-biscuit colour the effect was delightful.

She felt guilty, decking herself for an evening's entertainment when she should be calling Fede to say she must break their date that evening. But she kept putting it off, not sure what the right words might be. How could she possibly explain to him that she was standing him up to go to dinner with the Calvanis to see if he was one of them? No, whatever excuse she found, the truth was out of the question.

There was no putting it off any longer. She reached for the phone, but it rang before she could touch it.

'*Dulcie, cara.*'

'Hello,' she said, flooded with delight before she could get her defensive caution into position.

'I've been trying to find the courage to call you. You're going to be annoyed with me. I can't make it tonight, but it really isn't my fault.'

'You can't make it?' she echoed. She felt ridiculously disappointed, almost as though she hadn't been about to do the same thing herself.

'Something's come up. I can't get out of it.'

'Can't you tell me what it is?'

In the brief silence she sensed his unease. 'It's—complicated,' he said at last. 'I don't want to talk about it over the phone. You're not cross with me, are you?'

'Of course not,' she said, not entirely truthfully. 'It's just that I was looking forward to seeing you.'

'And I you. I'll call you tomorrow. *Ciao.*'

So that was that, she thought as she hung up. He'd made it easy for her. She should be glad. And she would be glad, just as soon as she'd silenced the little voice that said something was wrong. He couldn't tell her the real reason for his defection, and he hadn't worked out a convincing excuse.

Or perhaps he didn't think her worth a convincing excuse. He wouldn't call her tomorrow after all. This was the brush-off.

Stop being absurd, she told herself. He only did what you were planning to do. What's the difference?

But there was a difference, and a small dark shadow hovered over the evening ahead.

It should have been unalloyed pleasure. She was collected by a motor boat bearing the Calvani arms, and driven slowly along the Grand Canal just as the sun was sliding down the sky and turning the water to red. All around her Venice was settling in for the evening. Lights came on along the waterfront, bars and cafés buzzed with life, some gondoliers drifted home after a hard day while others emerged to start work on the late shift.

And then they were passing under the Rialto Bridge and there was the Palazzo Calvani, the whole great building ablaze with light. For a moment Dulcie had a glimpse of how it must have looked in its glory days, when Venice ruled the Adriatic, and palaces were alive with powerful men and glamorous women. It was a dream, of course. Reality had never been like that. But, looking at the gorgeous building, she could almost believe it.

And there was the count, resplendent in dinner jacket and snowy white shirt, looking as though he'd stepped out of that other age. Now she was glad that she'd dressed up in her gladdest of glad rags, and wouldn't feel out of place.

As the boat drew up at the landing stage he was there to assist her out, bowing low over her hand and declaring, 'You honour my house.'

Behind him were two fine-looking young men, both apparently in their early thirties. Neither looked remotely like the man she was investigating.

'My nephews, Marco and Leo.' Both young men greeted her with a flourish. 'You are very fortunate to find them here. Leo lives in Tuscany and Marco in Rome, but they came to see me when I became ill. My other nephew, Guido, lives with me all the time. He'll be here soon.'

So Guido was the one she needed to see, Dulcie thought. Alive to every nuance, she hadn't missed the way Leo and Marco had studied her without seeming to, and exchanged glances. They were gallantry itself, but the count outdid them both, brushing them aside to lead her out onto the terrace where he had ordered drinks.

From here the view was dazzling, not just the Grand Canal but the Rialto Bridge, bathed in floodlight. Dulcie looked a long time, awestruck by so much beauty.

'I see you understand my city,' the count said, smiling. 'You pay it the compliment of silence.'

She nodded. 'Words would only spoil it.'

'I linger here every night. It is best enjoyed alone

or—' he bowed '—with charming company. But I neglect your comfort. What will you drink?'

She accepted a wine that he recommended and returned to studying the view. Although the balcony looked out over the water she could see grounds to either side of it, ending in trees and shadows.

Then it seemed that one of the shadows moved, but the impression vanished in an instant.

'Is something the matter?' Francesco asked.

'No, I just thought I saw someone move down there. I must have been mistaken.'

They looked down into the gardens, but all was still and silent.

A last-minute phone call from an important customer meant that Guido was later reaching the palace than he'd meant to be, and arrived in jeans and sweater. Knowing this would incur his uncle's censure he slipped into the garden by a small gate to which only the initiated had the key, and moved quietly through the growing shadows. With luck he could reach his own room and change quickly into what Francesco called 'the proper attire' and what he called 'stuffed shirt.'

Through the trees he could discern the terrace overlooking the water, where the count would be entertaining their guest to pre-dinner drinks. Yes, he could see him now, also Leo and Marco, but the lady was still obscure. He could just make out that she was wearing an ice-blue dress, but not her face. It would be useful to discover more of her and know the worst that awaited him this evening. As he emerged from the trees he hugged the wall, flattening himself against it as he edged nearer the terrace.

There was a flash of pale blue as she turned to look outwards, and suddenly he saw her face clearly.

For a split second he froze with shock. Then he moved fast. It was too late to return to the trees. The only concealment lay directly under the terrace. A swift dash, and he just made it.

'Is something the matter?' he heard his uncle ask over his head.

Then Dulcie's voice. 'No, I just thought I saw someone move down there. I must have been mistaken.'

Guido's brow was damp. This couldn't be happening to him! What had become of his famous luck that had protected him through a thousand scrapes? Creditors— he'd paid them all eventually, but his early days in business had involved much tap-dancing—ladies with marriage in their eyes, husbands with shotguns, he'd sidestepped them all with wit and charm.

But where was his guardian angel now? Absent without leave, that was where. Another few minutes and he'd have walked in on Dulcie and his family, to be introduced in his true identity. It was no use saying that he'd meant to tell her soon anyway. He hadn't meant it like this.

Muffled noises from above, Leo and Marco voices, then his uncle's, irritated. 'What's happened to the fellow? My apologies for my nephew's tardiness. Call him one of you and ask when he'll be here.'

Guido moved fast to switch off his mobile before it could ring and reveal his location. He mopped his brow.

Marco spoke. 'His phone is off.'

'No matter,' Francesco declared. 'He'll be here at any moment.'

Not on your life! Guido thought desperately.

'I do hope so.' That was Dulcie. 'Because I'm really looking forward to meeting your third nephew, count…'

Their voices faded.

With calamity staring him in the face, Guido thought fast. Nobody had seen him. He could still get away. His mind was racing. Slip out the way he'd come in, call his uncle to apologise for the unexpected crisis that would prevent him having the pleasure of joining them tonight. Then tap-dance like mad.

He was about to begin his journey back through the garden when a truly appalling thought turned his bones to jelly.

He knew his uncle's routine with new guests. It never varied. Dinner, then a tour of the palace, finishing in his study. There he would produce his photo albums and display family pictures in which Guido would feature prominently.

He groaned aloud, wondering what he'd ever done to deserve this. But the list was too long to contemplate. At all costs Dulcie mustn't be allowed to see those pictures.

Backing against the wall he encountered a small door that he knew was never used. If he could get through he would be in a passage that led past the kitchen to the rear of the house and from there it was just a step to his uncle's study.

As he'd expected, the door was locked, but the wood was so old that a thump from a stone splintered it easily. The passage was pitch-black and he had to grope his way along, stumbling on the uneven floor, and once actually falling. He picked himself up, sensing that he was covered in dirt, but he had no time to worry about that. There was a light up ahead. The kitchen would be busy tonight and he must get past the door without being seen.

It took five minutes anxiously waiting for the right chance to present itself, and then he had to take a flying leap. Then he was in a narrow corridor, at the end of which was a secret door. By pressing the right knob he could make a section of the wall revolve, and bring himself into the study. The device had been installed in the seventeenth century by a count who feared assassination. Guido felt assassination might be a merciful end compared with what faced him if he couldn't get those photo albums.

His luck held. The study was empty and dark. The less light the better, so he put on just one small lamp and went to the desk drawer where his uncle kept the key to the glass-covered bookcase where the albums were kept. Moving quietly he knelt down and began to turn the key in the lock.

'Freeze!'

The voice came from behind him. He took a deep breath, hoping against hope that the cold metal he could feel against his ear wasn't what he thought it was.

'Stand up and turn around slowly with your hands up.'

He did so and found his worst fears realised as he stared down the length of a double-barrelled shotgun.

As the minutes ticked past with no sign of the missing heir the count's smile became glassy, until at last he announced that dinner could wait no longer. The four of them entered the vast, ornate dining room where Dulcie was escorted to the place of honour.

Francesco reminisced about Lady Harriet, with many anecdotes which Dulcie was sure he'd either invented or transposed from other ladies. Now and then he reverted to the bachelor theme.

'I keep hoping my nephews will marry and comfort me in my old age,' he mourned. 'But they're all stubborn and selfish.'

'Very selfish,' Leo agreed with a grin. 'We have this funny idea of marrying to suit ourselves rather than "serving the blood line".'

'I'm afraid we're all lonely bachelors in this family,' Francesco sighed.

'And your nephew Guido,' Dulcie asked. 'Is he a lonely bachelor?'

'Well, he's certainly a bachelor,' Marco observed.

His uncle gave him a look that would have cowed an easily frightened man.

'I must apologise to our guest for Guido's tardiness,' Francesco announced. 'But I have no doubt he will be here very soon.'

He raised his voice on the last words, as if sending a message to the delinquent to remind him of his duty. But no erring nephew materialised, and the three Calvanis exchanged glances, wondering where he could possibly be.

'Liza, please put that thing away,' Guido begged nervously. 'Here, let me take it.' He relieved the housekeeper of the shotgun and assisted her to a chair.

'It's not loaded,' she said faintly. 'I thought you were a burglar. *Maria vergine*! I might have killed you.'

'Not with an unloaded gun,' he pointed out. 'Although you nearly gave me a heart attack. And if I'd been a burglar what were you thinking of to tackle me like that? You've been watching too many gangster movies.'

'Yes,' she said with a sigh. 'I just thought a little excitement would be nice.'

'A little ex—? You need a restorative. Where does my uncle keep his best brandy? Here you are.' He handed her a glass, saying kindly, 'This will make you feel better. And if you want excitement, you can help me out of a spot I'm in. I need to get rid of these,' he indicated the albums. 'Just for a few hours.'

'But he always shows them to his guests,' Liza declared.

'I know, that's why I've got to make them vanish. I can't explain but a lot depends on it. In fact, everything depends on it. Liza, my whole future life is in your hands, my marriage, my children, my children's children, the whole Calvani blood line for the next hundred years. If you don't help me it's all finished. You wouldn't want that on your conscience, would you?'

'You're up to something.'

'Have you ever known me when I wasn't?'

'No. But you won't manage it this way. If he finds them missing he'll call the police.'

Guido tore his hair. 'Then what can I do?'

'Leave it to me, *signore*.'

Count Francesco was at his best when talking about the past glories of Venice, and although Dulcie recognised that it was a performance she still fell under its spell.

'Everyone came here for carnival,' he said expansively. 'It was a time for pleasure. You know, of course, why it's called carnival?'

'I'm afraid I don't,' she said. This was clearly the reply expected.

'It comes from *carne*, meaning flesh. Knowing that it would soon be Lent, a time of austerity, people revelled in the pleasures of the flesh, preferably from behind the safety of a mask. The orgies continued right up until Shrove Tuesday and stopped on the stroke of midnight.'

'So that's why Carnival is in February,' Dulcie said.

'The February carnival is a modern revival, designed to attract tourists during the winter. But who can make merry in the cold? I mark carnival in my own way, with a masked ball in summer. This year's ball will take place next Wednesday, and I hope you will honour me by attending.'

'Well, I'm not quite certain if I'll still be here next week,' she murmured.

'Oh, but you must,' he said earnestly, 'if only to spare my blushes about tonight. I don't know how to apologise for Guido's reprehensible behaviour in not turning up. I shall inform him of my displeasure.'

'But you've already done that,' Dulcie smiled, 'when he telephoned to apologise, half an hour ago. I'm disappointed not to have met him, but since this was a last-minute arrangement it must have been difficult for him.'

'You are most gracious to say so. But next week he will make his apologies in person.'

There was no turning him from this idea, so Dulcie murmured something vague and polite, and gave herself up to the enjoyment of the palazzo. When the guided tour was at an end they all drank brandy and coffee, and then the three men accompanied her to the landing stage where the boat was waiting. Leo and Marco would have taken her hand but the Count waved them away with an imperious gesture.

'To assist a beautiful lady is *my* privilege,' he said with old-world courtesy. '*Buona notte, signorina.* I'm sorry the evening wasn't more satisfactory. I'd hoped to show you my photo albums. I can't understand how my housekeeper came to lose the key. It's not like her to make such a mistake.'

'I shall look forward to seeing them another time,' Dulcie said.

'Yes, when you come to the masked ball. Next Wednesday. Don't forget. And Guido will be there.'

'I'm really looking forward to meeting him.'

The boatman settled her comfortably, and a moment later they were on their way down the Grand Canal. The Calvanis waved until she was out of sight.

'She's perfect,' the count said.

'Just the same uncle, you're barking up the wrong tree,' Leo observed.

'What do you mean?'

'Guido's romancing a new woman,' Marco said. 'It's the talk of Venice that he's spent all this last week with her, even taking days off work. When does Guido ever neglect his business? I tell you uncle, it's serious.'

'Why the devil didn't you tell me this before?'

'It seemed safer to get the evening over first,' Leo said.

'Is anything known about this woman?' Francesco demanded, in alarm.

'Only that he met her while he was rowing.'

Francesco snorted. 'A tourist, looking for a holiday romance, ready to disport herself with the first gondolier she meets. Lady Dulcie is a woman of *class*, and he neglects her for a floozie! Is he crazy?'

'He's a Calvani,' Leo observed.

The moon was high in the sky as Dulcie sat watching the Grand Canal drift by her. Venice was gently closing down for the night. The little waterside bars were emptying, and lights were going off. Now and then she could see a couple wandering by the water, arms entwined, then vanish into a *calle*, swallowed up by darkness the moment before their lips touched. A few gondolas were still drifting past, seeming to move from shadow to shadow. Every one of them seemed to contain lovers embracing, oblivious to the gondolier who grinned and looked over their heads. He'd seen so many lovers before.

But as far as Dulcie could see none of them was the man she was seeking, and she sighed, wondering what he was doing right now, what had kept him from her tonight, and how soon must she say goodbye to him? Perhaps he would call to say how much he'd missed her, and must see her. There might even be a message for her in the hotel.

She controlled her impatience, hurrying to the suite and fumbling with the key in her eagerness. But when she called the desk there were no messages. Dispiritedly she sat and stared at the telephone.

Suddenly she realised that she wasn't alone. There was a noise from the second bedroom, and the next moment the door opened.

'Jenny!' Dulcie exclaimed.

'Hello!' The young girl threw her arms about Dulcie in an eager greeting. 'It's so lovely to see you.'

'But what are you—I mean, I didn't know you were coming.'

'Dad said he thought we might enjoy a little vacation together. That's why he booked this suite, so that there'd be room for both of us.'

'Did he say why I was here?'

'Only that you were doing some market research for him. I know he's always expanding his business.'

It didn't seem to occur to Jenny to be suspicious, but then, Dulcie realised, she knew nothing about her work, and so there was no reason for her to think the worst. Yet Dulcie had a terrible feeling that things were going badly wrong.

'You look gorgeous,' Jenny said, surveying the evening dress. 'Oh, Dulcie, is it a man?'

'I've had dinner with three men, and none of them the one I wanted,' she said distractedly. 'Now I don't know whether I'm coming or going.'

'Three is too many,' Jenny said wisely. 'One is better, if it's the one you want. Oh, Dulcie, I'm so blissfully, blissfully happy. It was wonderful to see him again.'

Dulcie tensed. 'What was that?'

'When I arrived I called Fede straight away, from the airport, and he came to collect me, and we kissed and kissed. He said he'd missed me so much and then—'

'Wait a minute,' Dulcie said, trying to ignore the cold hand that clutched at her stomach. 'You've been with Fede this evening?'

'But of course. Who else? He didn't think he could make it at first—'

'But no doubt he changed his arrangements,' Dulcie said, her eyes kindling.

'I suppose so. I didn't ask. What does anything matter beside the fact that we're together?'

So that was where he'd been tonight, Dulcie seethed inwardly. He was playing fast and loose with the pair of them. And to think she'd been trying to see the best in him!

'Where are you going?' Jenny called as Dulcie strode to the door.

'Anywhere!' she flung over her shoulder.

As soon as she was out of the hotel she plunged into the maze of little dark streets. She didn't look where she was going. She didn't care. Jenny's innocent words had ripped the lid off the pretence that had sustained her for days. She'd read herself lectures about being on her guard, being professional, never quite trusting him. And all the time she'd been slipping under the oldest spell in the world.

It was dark in the *calles*. With only one light halfway along each one it was easy to stay out of sight, so she flattened herself against a wall, and stayed there as couples drifted past in the gloom, heard rather than seen, their voices low and full of emotion, fading into silence.

The city of lovers...

And she'd tumbled into its trap like a green girl who knew no better. Forewarned, forearmed, she'd still tumbled giddily into love while kidding herself that she was safe. Fool! Fool!

Serve me right, she thought defiantly. I'll know better next time.

But there couldn't be a next time, not quite like this. There might be other relationships, but never again would she feel the happiness and safety that had been like a blessing while he tended her. All an illusion. That was what hurt the most.

She moved further into the shadows, wondering if she would ever see a way out.

From his vantage point at a little bar across the Grand Canal Guido was able to watch Dulcie's departure. He leaned his arms on a rail as she went past in the boat, thinking how tragic it was to be so near and yet so far.

He allowed half an hour for safety before returning

home, even managing to whistle as he entered, only slightly out of tune.

So far, so good, but had his cover been blown? Liza had promised to 'lose' the key to the cabinet where the albums were housed, but suppose his uncle had a spare and had managed to take out the family snaps? There would be his face for Dulcie to recognise. Then she would have said—and Uncle Francesco would have replied—and there would have been a row—Leo and Marco would have roared with laughter—and now here he was heading for another row.

He considered emigrating. A snake-infested swamp might be nice. Or anywhere that was a long way away.

'There you are, you villain!'

The voice echoed down the long marble hall, followed by Francesco with a face like thunder, then Leo and Marco, determined not to miss the fun.

'Uncle, I can explain—' That was safely vague when you weren't quite sure what you were supposed to be explaining.

'Certainly you should explain, not to me but to that charming young lady. The way you've treated her is abominable.'

'That—depends on how you look at it,' Guido said, carefully feeling his way.

'That any nephew of mine—' Francesco broke off, fulminating, leaving Guido as much in the dark as ever. 'Get yourself in here.' He indicated his study which struck Guido as ominous.

The study was unrevealing. Wine glasses stood about, suggesting that everyone had spent some time in here, but the count took up his position in front of the cabinet, hiding the contents.

'She's a *lady*, do you realise that?' the count boomed.

'And you've behaved as though she were no more than—well, I don't know what to say!'

I wish you'd say a lot more, Guido thought. *Then I might get a clue.*

'She was charming about it,' Francesco went on. 'Oh, yes! Breeding tells, although she probably wants to hang you from the highest lamppost after what happened tonight.'

'What—exactly—happened tonight?' Guido asked.

'You ask me that?'

'Yes, I did actually. And you two—' Guido whirled on Leo and Marco '—can stop grinning or I'll have your hides.'

Had she seen the pictures or hadn't she? If he didn't find out soon he'd have a nervous breakdown.

'*Scusi signori.*' Liza had glided in like a ghost and began gathering wine glasses. Moving directly in front of Guido she gave him a brief thumbs up sign. He relaxed, but only a little.

'I'm sorry about tonight but something came up,' he said. 'And if, as you say, she was charming about it—'

'Lady Dulcie,' Francesco said with awful dignity, 'was naturally very disappointed not to have met you. She particularly asked me to tell you that.'

'Did she?'

'I also assured her that you would be at the masked ball, and she said how much she looked forward to meeting you there. She stressed that this meeting meant a great deal to her.'

In his eagerness to bring Dulcie and Guido together the count was gilding the lily, giving Dulcie's polite words a meaning they were never meant to bear. To Guido, his nerves already jangling, they sounded ominous. Clearly Dulcie had discovered the truth, but in-

stead of denouncing him she was keeping her wrath for
their next meeting. This was her message to announce
the approach of doom.

'Er—I think perhaps—excuse me, Uncle, something
else has come up.'

He got out as fast as he could.

CHAPTER EIGHT

IT WAS a mile to the Vittorio if you knew the backstreets well. Guido dodged and dived, taking a short cut that led through the house of a friend called Enrico, pilfered a glass of Enrico's wine and a kiss from Enrico's wife, before vanishing, calling his thanks over his shoulder.

A few minutes short of the hotel he found himself beside a small canal. Hurrying along, he nearly collided with a woman coming the other way.

'I'm so sorry—*Dulcie*! I—'

But her face told him the worst, and her words confirmed it.

'You are the lowest of the low,' she flung at him.

'If I could just explain—'

'What is there to explain? Only that you're a devious rat, and that I know already.'

'*Dio mio*! You did see them.'

'See what?'

He tore his hair. 'I wouldn't have had this happen for the world—'

'Then why do it? Oh, of course, you meant being found out. I suppose you thought I'd never discover the truth about you—'

'I was going to tell you myself, I swear I was.'

'And that was going to make it all right?'

'Of course not but—if I could make you understand how it came about. It was an accident. I know I should have told you everything from the start, but does it really matter so much. Just one tiny little deception—'

'*One tiny little*—? I don't believe you said that. I should have known when you stood me up tonight, giving a very fishy excuse, in fact no excuse at all. Something came up! Surely you could have managed something better than that?'

'I couldn't think of anything,' he admitted. 'But now you know, can't we start again?'

'Am I hearing things? Even you couldn't be so devious and unscrupulous—'

'*Cara*, please, I know I don't measure up to your high standards, but I will. I swear I will. Did I really do something so terrible?'

'If you have to ask that you wouldn't understand the answer. There's no point in talking any more. Goodnight, and goodbye.'

'You mustn't leave now. Stay and listen to me.' In his eagerness he took hold of her shoulders.

'I don't want to stay, and please let go of me.'

'I can't just let you go.'

'You can't do anything else. Take your hands off me.'

'Just another few minutes,' he begged.

'What kind of fool do you take me for? Let go.'

She tried to thrust her way past him, but he dropped his hands to her waist and drew her close.

'I'll let go,' he said firmly, 'when I've explained *this*.'

She tried to escape. This kind of 'explanation' was too dangerous. But his lips were unexpectedly fierce on hers. He was kissing her like a man whose life depended on it, as if he feared he might never get the chance again, and there was a forcefulness in his lips and his arms that thrilled her even while she fought to stay aloof.

She could feel the treacherous excitement creeping

through her. Her heart and sensations cared nothing for the warnings of her head. They wanted him, wanted what was happening now, wanted it to continue…

'Let me go,' she gasped, managing to free her mouth.

'I can't do that,' he said, also gasping. 'I daren't in case I never find you again. I won't risk that.'

'You've already lost me. I was never yours in the first place—'

He silenced her in the only way possible. It wasn't fair, she thought wildly. She'd fought this temptation since the moment she'd met him, and now he was forcing her to feel it when he'd just come from Jenny.

The thought of Jenny gave her the courage she craved. Putting out all her strength she managed to free herself. He took a step back, fighting to keep his balance while she fended him off. Neither of them realised they were standing so close to the water until he toppled in with a yell and an almighty splash.

Venetians live in and out of the water from their earliest years, and for one of them to fall into a canal is no big deal, except for the pollution. Guido kept his mouth firmly closed until he broke the surface, then rubbed his eyes and looked around for steps. But there were none in sight, and since it was low tide the stone bank was too high for him to climb out.

He reached up his hand, calling, 'Help me out, *cara*.'

Dulcie had dropped to one knee and was regarding him anxiously. 'Are you hurt?'

'No, but I'm wet. Help me out.'

'Why? You can swim!'

'Sure, I'm a great swimmer—'

'Good. Then swim home.'

She rose to her feet and turned away.

'*Cara!*'

Before his horrified eyes she vanished into the darkness, leaving him bobbing in the water.

It took another hour's walking before Dulcie had talked herself back into a sensible frame of mind. So he was a treacherous creep. She'd always known that. It was what she'd come here to prove. Now she'd done so, earned her fee, and she was very happy. The feel of his lips was still on hers, telling her she was lying to herself, but she would be strong-minded about it.

In this mood she returned to the Empress Suite, having made up her mind to warn Jenny about him. She'd waited too long already. Firmly she knocked on Jenny's bedroom door.

'I need to talk to you,' she called.

Jenny's voice came from inside. 'Can't it wait until morning?'

'No, it's important.'

Strange muffled sounds reached her, and a grunt that had a masculine tone. Full of foreboding, Dulcie opened the door.

The room was in darkness, but in the silver light from the window she could see the huge double bed. On one side of it was Jenny, hastily clutching the sheet to her. On the other side was a suspicious bump.

Dulcie stared at that bump, disbelief warring with anger and misery. He'd not only played her false, but he'd rushed straight back here after their encounter by the canal.

'This really isn't a good time,' Jenny protested.

'I think it's a great time to expose a man as a cheat and a liar,' Dulcie said firmly, making for the far side of the bed and grabbing the sheet.

A pair of hands grabbed it back. She yanked. He

yanked. But she yanked harder, wrenching the bed-clothes right back to reveal the naked man beneath.

She had never seen him before in her life.

'This is Fede,' Jenny said in a small voice.

'*This*?' Dulcie stared. 'He's not Fede.'

'Yes I am,' the young man declared, trying to haul the sheet back and cover his embarrassment. Having succeeded, he politely offered her his hand. 'I am Federico Lucci. How do you do?'

'Very badly,' Dulcie said in a dazed voice. 'In fact I think I'm going slightly crazy. If you're Fede, who did I just throw into the canal?'

They both stared at her.

Dulcie turned away suddenly and went to stand in the window, looking out. She was beyond thought, and almost beyond feeling. Buried deep in her turmoil was something that might yet turn out to be happiness. It was too soon to say.

The other two seized the chance to get out of bed and put some clothes on. When she looked back Fede had switched on the light, and now things began to be clearer—and more confused.

In the picture Roscoe had shown her there had been two men, one playing the mandolin and singing to Jenny. Naturally she'd assumed this was Fede. The other man, sitting just behind them, was little more than a baby-faced boy. It had never occurred to her—or to Roscoe, she was sure—that he might be Fede.

Yet it seemed that he was.

Then who—?

It was Jenny who recovered her composure first. 'What do you mean?' she asked. 'Why have you been going about throwing people into canals?'

'Because he asked for it,' Dulcie said wildly. 'Because he—oh, no, he couldn't have.'

'Perhaps you have been too much in the sun?' Fede suggested kindly.

'Yes I was,' Dulcie admitted. 'I was very poorly and he looked after me. But I thought he was you—he was wearing your shirt—at least, it had your name on it—and rowing a gondola—'

'It sounds like Guido,' he said.

The name stunned her. She'd been hearing about Guido all evening. 'Guido who?'

'Guido Calvani. He's been my friend since we were at school. One day he'll be a count, but what he really likes best is rowing my gondola. So I let him borrow it, but he has to pretend to be me because he doesn't have a licence.'

Dulcie forced her limbs to unfreeze long enough to go to her purse and take out the photograph.

'Is that him? The one playing the mandolin?'

'That's Guido,' Jenny said. 'He's been a good friend to Fede and me. When I first came to Venice he used to do Fede's stints on the gondola so that we could be together.'

'We knew we were being followed,' Fede put in, 'so sometimes we'd all go out together, to confuse her Poppa.'

'You confused him all right,' Dulcie said, sitting down suddenly.

Jenny gave Dulcie a puzzled look. 'But how do you come to have this picture?'

'Your father gave it to me,' Dulcie said reluctantly. 'As you suspected, he had you followed when you were last here. He thought Fede was—well—'

'A fortune hunter,' Fede supplied wryly.

'I'm afraid so, but it's worse. He seems to have got you totally muddled with Guido, and thinks you claimed to be heir to a title.'

'That's what Guido was telling me when that picture was taken,' Jenny remembered.

'Your father's spy must have been near enough to hear that,' Dulcie said, 'but not near enough to get the story straight. He obviously just overheard bits. Did he take this picture?'

'No, it was taken by one of the street photographers to sell to tourists,' Fede said. 'I know because I bought a copy off him, and one seems to have reached the count, Guido's uncle, and he's been giving him a hard time about it ever since. Signor Harrison's spy must have bought one too, and carried back a garbled version of what he'd overheard.'

Jenny was looking at Dulcie curiously. 'But why did Dad give this picture to you?'

'Can't you guess?' Dulcie said bitterly. 'I was sent here to find Fede and set him up.'

'How?'

'Pretend to be rich, divert his attention from you. Find out if he really was an aristocrat, as he's supposed to have claimed.'

'But I'm not,' Fede said blankly. 'I've never pretended to be. That's Guido.'

'I know that now. I was supposed to make a play for Guido—Fede—flaunt my money—Roscoe's money—then show you that he wasn't faithful, that he'd follow the cash. I'm a private detective, Jenny.'

'You're a *what*?'

'Your father hired me to ''open your eyes''. It seems that he's the one who's blind. Oh, Jenny, I'm so sorry.

I thought I was saving you from a deceiver. But I got it all wrong.'

She braced herself for the shock and disillusion in Jenny's eyes. But after the first moment Jenny relaxed and shrugged. As she looked at Fede a smile came over her face, and the next moment they were in each other's arms.

Dulcie understood. Jenny had the love of the man she loved, and nothing else mattered.

'You mean you've been sweet-talking the wrong man all this week?' she asked from the shelter of Fede's embrace.

'Something like that,' Dulcie said stiffly.

Jenny gave a choke of laughter, and Fede joined her. After a moment Dulcie too managed a weak smile.

'It's not funny,' she said. 'He's been deceiving me.'

'Well, you were deceiving him too.'

'Only in a good cause,' Dulcie said firmly. 'But I don't understand about this title. I've been to his home. It's in a backwater. It's not—'

'Not what you'd expect from a future count,' Fede supplied. 'That's why Guido likes it. Actually he's a very rich man in his own right. He started a business making souvenirs. He owns two factories, one making glass, and one making all sorts of tourist knick-knacks, fancy dress, pictures, videos—'

'Masks?' Dulcie asked in a strange voice.

'Oh, yes, masks. They're his speciality. He even designs some of them himself, but mostly he's a very sharp businessman. His official home is in the Palazzo Calvani, but he keeps that little apartment as a refuge, and of course it's a good place to take the kind of ladies he doesn't want his uncle to know ab—' he stopped as Jenny kicked him.

'Thank you,' Dulcie said blankly. 'I get the picture.'

'It's a pity you didn't hit on the right man,' Jenny mused.

'Pardon?' Fede was startled. 'You *want* other women chasing me?'

'Only because I know you'd have been faithful, my darling,' she told him fondly. 'Then Dulcie could have straightened the whole thing out with Dad.'

'I'm not sure I could,' Dulcie said. 'He wants you to marry a rich man, or a title, preferably both.'

'And all I want is Fede,' Jenny said. 'I don't care if I never see a penny of Dad's money. I'm of age. I don't have to do what he says. It's just that I wanted to avoid a split with him. You see, he's terribly stubborn. Once he's "cast me off" he'll feel he has to stick to it forever. And I'm all he's got. If we have a break he'll never see his grandchildren and he'll have a miserable, grumpy old age.'

'He's very set on having his own way about this,' Dulcie said.

'So am I.' For a moment Jenny's face looked astonishingly like Roscoe's. 'So we just have to think of something.' She yawned. 'But let's do it in the morning.'

'It *is* the morning,' Dulcie said. 'It's five o'clock.'

'There's plenty of night left,' Jenny said firmly. 'Goodnight, Dulcie. You should go and get some rest.'

Dulcie could only go to her own room and strip off, trying to come to terms with her turbulent thoughts. Part of her was furious with Guido. This was all his fault for pretending to be Fede when he must have known he wasn't, she thought illogically.

But part of her was gloriously happy because he wasn't a heartless schemer after all. All the best of him was true, the gentle consideration he'd shown her in his apartment, the chivalrous way he'd kept his distance while delicately hinting that he wanted something very different. It wasn't the calculation of a man pursuing a woman's fortune. It was the honest behaviour of a man who didn't need her fortune.

Her heart sank a little when she considered her own actions. But they had fooled each other, and surely they could put that behind them?

She'd been holding back her feelings, but now there was nothing to stop her admitting her love, and the world was bright again. At last she fell into a deep sleep which lasted until nine the next morning. She rubbed her eyes, wondering what the day would bring.

She showered and dressed hurriedly. As she left the bedroom she saw that breakfast had been served on the terrace. Jenny and Fede were sitting there drinking coffee, and they hailed her with smiles.

'Isn't it a wonderful morning?' Jenny said blissfully. 'I'm so happy I could die.'

'Then I will die with you,' Fede said gallantly.

'We'll all die if Roscoe gets wind of this,' Dulcie said, but she too was happy. Guido was a free man. The delicate emotion that had built up between them over the last few days was love after all, and she was free to give her feelings full rein. If only she could see him soon.

There was a knock on the door.

'I ordered more coffee for you,' Jenny said.

'Thanks, I'll answer it,' Dulcie said, rising and making her way to the outer door, where someone outside was knocking again, impatiently.

She pulled it open and saw Guido.

Mingled with her first leap of joy was amusement at

his expression. He looked definitely sheepish, and entered cautiously, as though expecting boiling oil to fall on him. Remembering their last meeting Dulcie wondered if she herself should be looking for boiling oil.

'You're not still mad at me?' he asked, studying her smiling face.

'Should I be?' she fenced.

'Well, you were pretty mad last night. I should remember because you threw me into the water.'

'I didn't throw you, you tripped.'

'You didn't help me out.'

'You can swim.'

'And I had to. In the end I got picked up by a barge carrying garbage and I got home smelling so bad even the alley cats fled from me. It's not funny,' he added as her lips twitched.

'Yes, it is.'

'Yes, I guess it is,' he conceded wryly. 'When I awoke today I knew I had to see you and explain, try to make you understand how it happened—but now— all that really matters is—' he became absorbed in watching her face '—all that matters—kiss me, my darling, *kiss me!*'

He pulled her against him in the same moment that she opened her arms to him. She knew now how badly she'd longed for the feel of his lips on hers. She'd pretended it wasn't true, but secretly she'd ached for him to kiss her.

'I've wanted to do this so often,' he murmured between kisses. 'I knew from the first moment that it was you, and you knew it too, didn't you, *cara*?'

'I don't know what I knew,' she whispered, dazed.

'You did, you must have done.' He kissed her again

and again. 'So many kisses to make up,' he said against her mouth. 'And all our lives for more kisses.'

'All our—?' She could hardly believe what she was hearing. Everything was going too fast.

'Of course. Years and years to spend kissing you and loving you in every possible way. Years to have beautiful children with you.' He pulled back, taking her head gently between his hands, and she never afterwards forgot the sight of his face, gloriously happy, blazing with triumphant love. It lived in her mind as a terrible contrast to what followed.

'Tell me, darling,' he said crazily, 'do you believe in Fate?'

'Well, I—'

'Because it was Fate, wasn't it, that brought us together, Fate that made your sandal fall off straight into my boat?'

'Not exactly,' she said, beginning to see danger.

'It wasn't an accident?' he asked, eyes wide. Suddenly he burst into joyful laughter. 'You saw me from the bridge, and you said to yourself, "I must have this handsome fellow", so you tossed your shoe to get my attention. Oh, *cara*, say that it's true. Think what it will do for my ego.'

'Your ego is quite big enough without help,' she countered, playing for time. '"This handsome fellow" indeed!'

'Last night when you were angry I thought my life was over.' Abruptly his tone changed and he spoke in a moved voice that startled her. 'Because that's what you are to me. My life.'

'But you don't know me—'

'I knew you from the first moment. I know you have a kind heart and will forgive my innocent deception, because you know it didn't spring from malice. But tell me, how did you find out? I was going to ask you last night, but you were too busy throwing me into the canal.' With his mercurial nature he'd gone from serious to clowning in a split second. Dulcie could barely keep up with him.

'I don't blame you for ducking me,' he hastened to add. 'When you found out I wasn't whom you thought—how did you find out by the way?'

'I didn't, not until later.'

'But—then why were you mad at me? I'm not an unreasonable man, *cara*, but when someone throws me into the canal I like to know why.'

'Does it matter?' she asked, finding his fun irresistible, even at this fraught moment. 'I should think Venice is full of people who'd like to throw you into canals.'

'Sure to be. But they usually control it.'

What a life it would be with this enchanting madman, she thought. If only she could navigate the shoals ahead first.

'Listen,' she said urgently, 'I've got something to tell you—'

'Tell me that you love me,' he broke in. 'Tell me that first and last and what do I care for anything else? You do love me, don't you?'

'Yes, yes, I do. But listen to me, it's important—'

'Nothing is important except that we've found each other. Kiss me, now and always—'

She was in his arms again, her troubled words silenced by his lips, and this time it was different, as though her confession of love had invigorated him. Before, his embrace had been troubled, cautious, asking her response. Now he was a man who knew himself loved and it was there in the possessiveness of his mouth and his arms. She would tell him everything in a moment, she promised herself, but just a moment— and another moment—

'Is that the coffee?' came a call from the next room.

'A curse on anyone who interrupts us,' Guido sighed. 'We shall have to go and be polite *carissima*, but soon we must be alone together, and then—'

There was another shout from inside and Guido reluctantly let her go.

'Later,' he whispered, then raised his voice to call, 'Fede,' and went in search of the voice. 'What the devil are you doing here? And Jenny! How wonderful to see you again!'

Dulcie followed him into the main room to find him laughingly embracing Jenny.

'You two know each other?' he said, looking from Jenny to Dulcie.

'Only slightly,' Dulcie said quickly.

'Guido my friend, I was going to call you and beg your help,' Fede said quickly.

'You two don't look as if you need my help. I never saw two lovers so happy.'

'But Jenny's Poppa still wants to break us up. He even put a private detective on our trail to discredit me.'

Guido made a sound of disgust. 'A private detective? What kind of miserable apology for a human being deliberately chooses such a sneaky, underhand job? Still, what harm can he do you?'

There was an awkward silence. Dulcie took a deep breath.

'It's not a he,' she said. 'It's me.'

Slowly Guido turned to look at her.

CHAPTER NINE

'WHAT did you say?' Guido asked quietly.

It took all her courage to say, 'I'm the private detective.'

'You?' he sounded as though he didn't know what the words meant.

'But Dulcie is on our side now,' Fede said eagerly, 'so it's all right. She's going to help us.'

'I don't know if Roscoe will listen to me,' Dulcie said, 'but I'll do everything I can.'

Guido was gazing at her curiously, but his manner was still calm. He hadn't quite understood yet. Or maybe he didn't want to.

'You're—a private detective?' he repeated slowly, still in that strange way, as though he was trying to decipher meaningless sounds.

'Yes.'

'And you came here to—?'

'Roscoe's worried about Jenny. He got the wrong end of the stick. He thought Fede was claiming to be you.'

'Can you imagine that?' Fede chuckled. 'Me, related to a count! So he sent Dulcie to find me and tempt me away from my Jenny. As though anyone could do that. Only—here's the joke—she thought you were me!'

'And so she targeted me instead,' Guido said lightly. 'Yes, it's an excellent joke.' A light had gone out of him, not just from his eyes but from his whole being. 'So that's what it was all about.'

Jenny made a slight restless movement at an intonation she heard in Guido's voice. Fede, an innocent, was merely trying to put Guido in the picture without realising the implications. Jenny tried to attract his attention but he was in full flight.

'There aren't many who fool you, Guido,' he observed cheekily.

'Until today I'd have said none at all,' Guido responded at once. He raised Dulcie's hand to his lips. 'My congratulations, *signorina*. A wonderful masquerade, played out to the finish with utter conviction.'

'You got the better of him, Dulcie,' Fede said. 'Someone should give you a medal.'

'That will be my privilege,' Guido said quietly.

There was no anger or condemnation in his eyes. Just a puzzled look, as though he were wondering how the world could have changed in a moment. Dulcie ground her nails into her palm. If only she could have told him in her own words. Now he'd heard in the worst possible way.

'Perhaps,' she said carefully, 'you should wait until you know the whole story. There's so much you don't know—that I must explain—'

'A man never knows the whole of it,' he agreed. 'But enough to matter. Enough to cast a strange light over what he thought was true, and show it in very ugly colours.'

It was hard for her to answer, but before she could even try he'd given Jenny a friendly, reassuring smile, saying, 'So we have a problem. We have to solve it. That's all. At least you can tell your Poppa that Fede has made no false claims. That should please him.'

'You don't know my father,' Jenny said. 'When he takes "agin" someone, that's it.'

'And it's my poverty that really offends him,' Fede

said gloomily. 'When he knows the truth he'll want Jenny to marry you, and be a countess.'

'Don't worry,' Guido said lightly. 'I shall tell him I'm going to become a monk. Love is too complicated for me.' He turned to Dulcie. 'So you were sent here to delude us. Are you going to tell us your real name?'

'I've been using my real name,' she said, adding softly, 'unlike some people.'

He had the grace to redden, but recovered himself. 'But what's in a name?' he asked her. 'That isn't always where the truth lies.'

'Yes, there's also the work people do, and pretending to live one kind of life while actually living another.'

His eyebrows rose. 'You talk to me about a "pretend" life?'

That silenced her.

'Have you thought of anything yet?' Fede asked anxiously.

'Patience,' Guido adjured him. 'I've only just discovered how things really stand.' A tremor went through him, although his face still smiled. 'Even a genius like me can only think so fast.'

'It's hopeless,' Fede said, immediately plunged into gloom. 'Nothing can be done.'

'Why don't we ask Dulcie?' Guido suggested. 'After all, intrigue is her profession, and she does it surpassingly well.'

'No,' she said hastily. 'This is a Venetian intrigue, and my talents don't stretch to it.'

'You do yourself an injustice, *signorina*,' Guido assured her quietly. 'You have the Venetian gift for dodging around corners, looking at one fact, seeing another, and believing a third. It's a great skill and most outsiders never acquire it. You, I believe were born with it.'

'On the contrary, *signore*,' she said, meeting his eyes defiantly. She'd found her second wind now, and if this was the game he wanted to play, then he would find she could give as good as she got. 'You forget that I've recently been taking lessons from a master.'

'And I,' he murmured so softly that only she could hear, 'I, who thought I had nothing left to learn, have found differently.'

'Life is full of unexpected lessons,' she murmured back. 'People may be more innocent than they seem.'

'People may certainly be very different to how they seem,' he said, subtly twisting her words.

She nodded. 'For instance, you shouldn't trust someone who plays games.'

He shrugged. 'You could say that about everyone.'

'No, some of us have a living to earn.'

'Ah, yes,' he seemed much struck. 'When it's done for money it's so much more virtuous, is it not?'

Her eyes met his and found in them something unexpected. He was angry but he was also hurt and confused. This situation had caught him off balance, and he wasn't coping as smoothly as he tried to make out.

A moment later he rose, kissed Jenny's cheek, shook Fede's hand and said with a flourish, 'Bless you. I'm happy for you. And don't worry, I'll think of something. And you, *signorina*—' he turned to Dulcie '—it was a pleasure talking to you but now I must be going. I've been unaccountably neglecting my work recently and now there's a mountain of it awaiting me, that will occupy me for some time.'

He was gone without waiting for a reply, but she had none to make. What could she say to a man who so clearly wanted to get away from her?

*   *   *

At Guido's souvenir factory on the island of Murano his employees were becoming concerned. For several days their employer had been absent without warning. Once a day he'd called them, but then switched his phone off and was impossible to contact.

His return caused general relief, which soon turned to surprise. Guido had always run an efficient business, but he'd done so with good humour, teasing, and the occasional semi-flirtatious coaxing. No more. His orders were still given with courtesy, but coolly, crisply, like a man with no time to spare. When someone cracked a joke in his presence he looked blank, as though wondering what a joke was.

It took Dulcie a day to track him down, and as she walked into the factory she had a horrible suspicion that everyone there knew who she was and why she was here. But the young man in the entrance directed her upstairs without fuss.

On the top floor she found Guido's office, and through the windows that formed the walls she could see him there at his desk, talking to a middle-aged man. The man saw her and nudged Guido, making him look up.

His face startled her. It was tired and worn, as if he hadn't slept for an age and had forgotten how to smile. He glanced in her direction, then away, and for a dreadful moment she thought he would refuse to see her. But then he nodded and indicated for her to be shown in.

The inside of his office reminded her how little she really knew him. The computer, the multiple phone lines, the stacks of files, the walls covered in plans and diagrams, all these told her that this was a man who took his business seriously.

'Is this the real you?' she asked lightly.

'One of me,' he answered briefly. 'I'm surprised to find you still in Venice. I thought you'd have gone yesterday.'

'You know I didn't because you heard me knocking on your door last night.' She added quietly, 'I knocked for a long time before I went away.'

'It wasn't a good moment,' he said. 'I wouldn't have known what to say, especially in that place.' His eyes challenged her with memories of the few happy days they'd spent in the little apartment. Then he looked away and began to pace his office, never getting too close to her. 'But I'm glad you came to see me.'

'You are?' she asked hopefully.

'Yes, it's right that we should say goodbye properly.'

His coolly dismissive tone annoyed her. 'I'll say goodbye when I'm good'n ready, not when you tell me to. There's a lot more to be said first.' In a softer tone she added, 'I listened to you when you were making your excuses yesterday.' She added, 'And that's not all I listened to you saying.'

She regretted the words at once. If his face wasn't closed against her before it was now. She'd reminded him of what he didn't want to remember.

'It wasn't kind of you to bring that up,' he said. 'You should have laughed over your victory in private, not to my face.'

'Laugh over—? What are you saying? I'm not laughing. I never meant any of this to happen.'

'You never *meant*? Excuse me, I understood that you came to Venice deliberately, for a purpose.'

'But it had nothing to do with you,' she cried.

'Ah, yes, I'd forgotten. You came to deceive and ruin my friend, not me, which of course makes everything all right.'

'I came to protect Jenny from a fortune hunter.'

'And how could you be so sure he was a fortune hunter? Your information was hardly brilliant since you confused him with me.'

'The information was lousy,' she admitted. 'It came from Roscoe. But the idea was to find out if he was right.'

'He'd made up his mind before you started.'

'He had, I hadn't.'

He stopped pacing and spoke angrily, 'For pity's sake, what kind of woman does this? Is it how you get your kicks?'

'No, I do it to eat. I've got nothing. Roscoe paid for everything.'

He regarded her with what might almost have been a smile. 'Like a theatrical performance, really. Set and costumes courtesy of Roscoe Harrison, and script by— who? Did you cook it up between you?'

'It wasn't like that—'

'*Answer me*,' he said sternly. There was no trace in him now of the light-hearted young man who'd enchanted her. There was something grim in his manner that she wouldn't have believed without seeing it. 'Answer me,' he commanded again. 'How much of what happened between us was planned?'

'I came to seek out Federico. I thought it was you because of the picture.' She showed him the snapshot. 'Yes, I was looking for your face, but when I found you, you were wearing his shirt, with his name on it—'

'And how did you happen to find me?'

'I was searching for you,' she admitted.

He raised his eyebrows sardonically. 'So our very meeting wasn't the accident I thought. And that touching moment when your sandal fell at my feet in the gondola?'

The moment he'd called Fate, with shining eyes, full of love.

'I threw it,' she admitted in despair. 'I stood on the bridge hoping you'd look up, and when you didn't I tossed my sandal.'

She flinched, watching him. She no longer knew how this man would react to anything.

For the moment there was no reaction at all. Then abruptly he broke into laughter, that filled her with relief, until she heard the disturbing edge to the sound, not like real amusement at all.

'That's hilarious,' he said at last. 'You calculated the whole thing, down to the last detail, and the poor sap fell for it, hook, line and sinker. He even burbled something stupid about it being Fate. Or did he? Remind me. No, on second thoughts, don't remind me. There are some mistakes a man should be able to forget in peace.'

'But it wasn't just me, was it?' she said indignantly. 'When I saw the name on your shirt you could have said, "I'm not Fede, just a rich playboy, fooling about in a boat". Why didn't you?'

'I forget,' he said stonily.

'I don't think that's a truthful answer. You could have stopped everything right there and then. Why didn't you?'

'I've forgotten,' he repeated. 'All right, maybe I've only forgotten because I want to. Believe what you like, but most of all believe that it's best if you go away from here and never come back.'

'I'm not ready to give up and go yet.'

'That's a pity because I don't think Venice is big enough to hold both of us.'

The door was thrown open abruptly by a middle-aged woman, full of excitement, who gabbled something Dulcie didn't understand. Guido gave her a brief smile and replied tersely. The next moment she surged into the room, followed by two young girls, their arms filled with masks.

'No,' Guido started to say, but his protest was lost in the hubbub. He shrugged and gave up. 'Our new line,' he said to Dulcie, sounding harassed. 'We've been waiting for them, but this isn't the moment—oh, be damned to it!'

The masks were magnificent, not merely painted cardboard like the ones on his walls, but covered in satin and sequins, many with gorgeous feathers.

Guido admired them and spoke kindly to his employees, but managed to shoo them out of the room fairly quickly.

'Harlequin,' Dulcie said, holding up a creation in scarlet satin with multi-coloured feathers on top. 'And this one—' she lifted a long-nosed mask in purple satin, 'Pantalone, the merchant. I remember what you told me.'

'But there were other things I didn't have time to tell you,' Guido mused. 'About Columbine, for instance.'

'You said she was sensible, but sharp and witty, and could see the funny side of life.'

'I also said she's a deceiver. She teases and beguiles Harlequin, leads him into her traps, while all the while laughing up her sleeve because he's fool enough to believe in her. He, poor clown, ends up wondering what's hit him.'

He spoke lightly but she had a sensation of his pain that was almost tangible. She guessed that he wasn't used to unhappiness, his life had contained so little of it. Now he was floundering. She longed to reach out to him, but didn't dare.

'You told me I wasn't like Columbine,' she reminded him.

He smiled sadly. 'I was wrong. You think I'm unfair because we both deceived each other, but your deception was planned before you ever came here. That's what I can't get past. Mine was an impulse that I yielded to—stupidly perhaps, but on the spur of the moment because—well, no matter.'

'Tell me,' she begged. It was suddenly terribly important.

But he shook his head. 'It doesn't make any difference now. I wish it did. Go away, Dulcie. There's nothing so dead as a dead love.' His face contracted suddenly. 'For pity's sake, go,' he said harshly.

If she could have thought of any way of moving him she would have tried, even then, but there was about him a kind of wintry stubbornness that she couldn't fight. He'd grown older since yesterday.

His phone shrilled and he made a grab for it with a mutter of impatience. Dulcie turned to go, wondering if the end could really come like this. But she turned as Guido barked, '*Fede*!'

'What is it?' she asked with a feeling of foreboding.

He was talking in Venetian. Dulcie caught the word 'Jenny,' then Fede's name repeated several times as though Guido was trying to calm him down. Dulcie could just make out the tinny sound of a voice from the phone, and it sounded as though Fede was in a rare panic.

'What is it?' she said as Guido hung up.

He was snatching his jacket down from a hook.

'Come on,' he said, grasping her arm. 'We've got to hurry.'

They were out of the factory and by the waterside before she had breath enough to ask, 'What's happened?'

A motor boat was waiting with a man at the wheel. Guido helped her down into it and then they were roaring away across the lagoon, feeling the spray in their faces. He had to shout above the noise of the engine.

'Your employer has arrived.'

'My—you mean Roscoe?'

'Right. Jenny's Poppa. She managed to call Fede and he called me. We have to do something fast to stop him taking her back to England.'

'You promised Fede you'd think up a plan.'

'I'm thinking of one now. First we have to walk into the hotel together.'

'And say what?'

'I'm trying to work that out,' he said tensely. 'We must put this man straight about the facts, and for that I need you there.'

'So sometimes Harlequin needs Columbine's help?'

'Sometimes he can't do without her, even if he doesn't like it. It's time to make up your mind whose side you're on.'

'I'm on Jenny's side. You heard me tell them I'll help.'

Instead of answering he yelled something to the boatman, and their speed increased, so that further talk became impossible. Soon they'd reached the Grand Canal, and had to slow down dramatically.

'Can't we go any faster?' Dulcie asked.

'No, it's the law. There's the hotel.' As he handed

her out of the boat he said, 'We're going to have to put on a rare performance.'

'But what's the script?' she asked frantically.

'Play it by ear.' He was sweeping her through the lobby to the lift.

'But suppose we're using different ears?' she demanded as they reached the top floor.

'You're the one that's good at this.'

'Don't give me that. I'm an amateur. You could give me lessons.'

'All right, how's this? You know this man and I don't. You lead, I'll follow. Do it for Jenny. Do it for Fede whose life you tried to ruin.'

There was no time to answer. The lift door was opening. Ahead were the double doors of the suite, and from behind them came the sound of voices, Jenny's distraught, Fede's frantic.

Guido was looking at her expectantly.

'Here we go,' she said, throwing open the doors.

As entrances went, it was splendid. The three inside stared at them. Then Jenny rushed to her in appeal, Fede rushed to shake Guido's hand, babbling in Venetian. Dulcie fixed her eyes on Roscoe, who was red-faced and shouting, 'I don't know who this man is—' jabbing a finger at Fede.

'It's Fede,' Jenny protested.

'The hell he is!' Roscoe snapped.

'The hell he isn't!' This, from Guido.

'You—' Roscoe swung around to him '—you're the one who's caused all this trouble.'

For the first minute Dulcie's mind had been a blank, but now suddenly the clouds parted. She pulled herself together and spoke with apparent confidence.

'Mr Harrison,' she said, 'allow me to introduce

Signor Guido Calvani, nephew of Count Calvani, a family that I've now discovered was once well acquainted with my own.'

The mention of Dulcie's family made Roscoe pause, as she'd hoped. It gave her time to rush on, 'It was only after I arrived here that I realised the significance of the name Calvani. It turns out that my great-aunt, *Lady Harriet*, knew Guido's uncle very well, if you know what I mean,' she managed a coy simper, 'and *the count* welcomed me most warmly when I visited his *palazzo* yesterday.'

She was laying it on with a trowel, stressing the words that would send signals to Roscoe's snobbery, and every one of them was hitting the bull's eye, she was glad to see.

True to his promise to follow her lead Guido wrung Roscoe's hand and said all the right things at length. Then he said them again at even greater length. Roscoe managed a reasonably civilised reply, but then became himself again.

'But you're in that picture making up to my daughter.'

'But only under the eye of her true love,' Guido said quickly, drawing Fede forward. 'I gather you've already met my friend, Federico Lucci, who's been fortunate enough to win Jenny's affection.'

'Now wait,' Roscoe blustered, 'what were you doing in that outfit? That's why I thought you were Fede—'

'He's Fede,' Guido said. 'I'm Guido.'

'*Count* Guido?'

'Not while my uncle lives, which hopefully will be many years yet.'

'But you—' Roscoe looked from Guido to Fede and from Fede to Dulcie '—you—no, wait—'

Then inspiration came to Dulcie in a blinding flash.

'Mr Harrison, pretty soon you and I need to discuss this fiasco,' she said, sounding slightly truculent. 'How am I supposed to do a decent job of work when your briefing to me was so inaccurate?'

He gaped. 'I—'

'Look at this picture.' She produced the snapshot. 'You assured me that the man with the mandolin was Federico Lucci. On that basis I allocated you a portion of my time which, let me remind you, doesn't come cheap. And after a week when I've given you my best efforts, I discover that ''Fede'' was really the other man, and I've been on a wild-goose chase.'

'But you said you knew him,' Roscoe hollered.

'I said no such thing. I said my family knew his, way back. He could have been anybody for all I knew. I've been glad to make contact with the count, who once knew Lady Harriet, but apart from that the whole thing has been a waste of time, for which I hold you entirely to blame.'

'OK, OK, maybe I got it a bit wrong,' Roscoe said in a placating voice, 'but it hasn't been a *total* waste of time. We've established that *he*—' indicating Fede '—is no aristo.'

'Since he never claimed to be, that's hardly surprising,' Dulcie said briskly. 'Can we drop this nonsense now? I've established that the man your daughter loves isn't trying to beguile her with false claims, which is surely what really matters.'

Roscoe was uncharacteristically hesitant. His slow-moving wits had taken in that Guido was a real 'aristo' and therefore to be cultivated, and that Fede was his friend. To have repeated his suspicions of Fede without offending Guido would have taken social skills Roscoe didn't possess. He fell silent, fuming. Guido divined what was going through his mind, and stepped into the breach, all charm.

'I know that my uncle would be anxious to extend to you his hospitality,' he said smoothly. 'He's giving a fancy-dress masked ball next week, and your presence, with your daughter, would make it complete.'

Roscoe's snobbery warred with his desire to hasten Jenny back to England. Snobbery won.

'That's generous of you,' he bawled. 'We'd like that, wouldn't we, pet? That's very—well, I must say—'

Under cover of his noisy pleasure, Guido murmured to Dulcie, '*Brava*! Columbine has worked her magic. You knew just how to deal with him.'

'He was getting on my wick,' Dulcie said crisply.

Roscoe had recovered himself and was wringing Guido's hand. 'Tell your uncle I'll come to see him right away. Men of substance should stick together—'

'My uncle is away just now,' Guido improvised hastily, 'but he will have the pleasure of your acquaintance at the ball.' He turned swiftly to Dulcie before Roscoe could think of any more tortures for him. 'I understand that you will be there, *signorina*. It will be delightful to see you. Fede, let us leave.'

'But I—' the hapless Fede started to say.

'Not now,' Guido said through gritted teeth, urging him out with more vigour than gentleness. 'For pity's sake, my friend, quit while you're ahead.'

CHAPTER TEN

GUIDO had prevented Roscoe taking Jenny away, thus buying the lovers some time, but the strain of the ensuing days nearly turned Dulcie's hair white.

He moved into the suite, taking over the second bedroom so that Jenny and Dulcie had to share the first. He spent his time exploring the city, dragging his daughter along, and proud to bursting point of having Lady Dulcie as his guide.

He demanded a full account of her dinner at the *palazzo*, with diversions regarding the social niceties to be observed at a count's residence.

'Just because I'm a self-made man it doesn't follow that I'm an ignoramus,' he declared belligerently. 'And I don't want any mistakes in that direction.'

Dulcie assured him that nobody could possibly make any mistakes.

Guido telephoned her once, explaining coolly that the best masquerade outfits were to be found at a shop in the Calle Morento. She should take Jenny there and make sure she chose a Columbine costume.

'Shouldn't that be me?' she asked wryly.

'On no account. They have a wide choice and I'm sure you'll find something suitable, but definitely not Columbine. But please tell Jenny that if all goes well she'll be with Fede from then on.'

'You're planning for them to run away that night?'

'I'm planning a little more than that, but everything has to be done just right.'

'Do I have any part to play?'

'Yes, and I'm sure you'll play it superbly when the time comes.'

But you don't trust me enough to tell me now, she thought.

'A lot depends on your following my instructions exactly,' Guido continued. 'Put yourself in the assistant's hands, she knows your requirements.'

'I suppose you have a connection with the shop?'

'I own it,' he said with some surprise.

'Of course.'

That was her only contact with him. There wasn't another word, and she was too proud to seek him out again. Although he wanted her to stay, he hadn't relented. She would be useful in his plan to help Jenny and Fede. That was all.

It was hard to believe that the magical web that had been spun between them during those few precious days could have been wrecked so easily: harder still to realise that the gentle jester who'd nursed and protected her was also the austere man who judged her harshly.

And unreasonably, she reminded herself. Her deception might have been greater than his, but he could have sorted it all out in a moment. Instead he'd let her mistake pass because—because of what? Something he couldn't bear to tell her. She might guess, but it was better not to, because then the ache of 'might-have-been' started all over again.

She'd thought that Simon had left her unhappy, but now she could see that misery in proportion. He'd been a skunk all the time and she was well rid of him. She'd known that even while she suffered. But Guido was different. She'd fallen deeply in love with him during those few precious days alone, and now that he'd changed towards her she couldn't dismiss it as a lucky escape. He was the one. Unlikely as it seemed there had been truth between them, concealed, perhaps, by masks, but he himself had said, 'when people's faces are hidden they are free to become their true selves.'

If only things had been different, how they could have enjoyed discovering their own and each other's true selves. It could have been the work of a lifetime.

Now there was nothing, and a fearful blank facing her. She couldn't persuade this man because she didn't know him. And the new Guido, curt, withdrawn, unreachable, was an alarming man.

As he wanted she took Jenny to the hire shop. Roscoe insisted on accompanying them, and chose a lavishly bejewelled Henry VIII costume for himself. Dulcie beat off his efforts to dress her as Anne Boleyn, but then he insisted on Cleopatra, which she felt was almost as bad.

Jenny went through this in a dream, following Guido's instructions as relayed by Dulcie, but without conviction. With her father's arrival her confidence seemed to have drained away. Despite her brave words about being of age and pleasing herself she reacted to Roscoe like a rabbit trapped in headlamps. Sometimes she managed to telephone Fede, but the conversations were always hurried affairs and she usually had to hang up quickly.

'Stand up to your father,' Dulcie insisted one evening. 'Tell him you're going to marry Fede and that's it. Or just walk out.'

'You make it sound so easy,' Jenny sighed.

'It is easy.'

'It would be for you. You're not afraid of anyone or anything.'

I'm afraid of my future, Dulcie thought. It's looking bleak and lonely right now.

'Dulcie, what am I going to do? You say Guido's going to make everything right, but how? If it doesn't work, Dad's going to haul me off home. I can't see Fede, I can only call him for a minute at a time. Dad watches me like a hawk.'

'Write Fede a letter,' Dulcie said at once. 'I'll take it to him.'

'You'd do that for me? Oh, thank you.'

'Write it now. Will Fede be rowing tonight?'

'I don't know,' Jenny said, scribbling hurriedly. 'But I'll give you his family's address.'

In a couple of minutes the letter was being sealed in an envelope, and Dulcie was hurrying out, hoping to avoid Roscoe, but failing.

'Where are you going?' he boomed. 'It's time to go out to dinner.'

'I'll join you later. I've got something to do first.'

'Don't be late.'

She had to consult a map to find the tiny Calle Marcello, well away from the tourist haunts. Darkness was falling, lights blazed from the grocery shops that were still open, and from the rooms overhead.

She found the little alley and almost walked past no: 36. The door was dark and easy to miss. She hesitated before knocking, suddenly shy. From inside she could hear sounds of movement, cheerful voices, laughter. She knocked.

The door was opened by Guido.

For a moment they stared at each other. Dulcie found no softening in his face, only a dismay as great as her own.

'I came to see Fede,' she said at last. 'Is he here?'

'Sure,' he said briefly, and stood aside for her to pass.

'Who's that?' came a hearty female voice from deep in the house.

The next moment its owner came into view. She was large, middle-aged and had a ruddy, smiling face, flushed from cooking.

'*Ciao*!' she boomed.

'This lady is English, Maria,' Guido said. 'She wants to see Fede.'

'Aha! You know my son?'

'A little,' Dulcie said hastily. 'I have a letter for him, from Jenny.'

Maria screamed with delight. 'You are a good friend. I am Maria Lucci.'

'I'm Dulcie,' she gasped, swallowed up in the woman's embrace.

'*Si*. I know. Lady Dulcie.'

'No,' she said hastily. 'Just Dulcie.'

Maria bawled, '*Fede*!' and urged Dulcie towards an inner door. 'You go through there. We just start eating. You eat with us.'

'Oh, no, I don't want to intrude,' she said hastily. It was unnerving to have Guido standing there in silence. 'I'll just give him the letter and go.'

'No, no, you eat with us,' Maria insisted. She stomped away, bawling something in dialect that Dulcie guessed was a demand for an extra chair.

'You have to stay,' Guido said quietly. 'When a Venetian family asks you into their home it's an honour. We're not like the English who just go through the forms.'

'But you don't want me to stay, do you?' she challenged.

'That means nothing. This isn't my home.'

'No, you never honoured me with an invitation to your home.'

'But I did. I took you to my real home, the home of my heart. There I thought I began to know your heart, which only proves what a fool I am.'

Dulcie was in despair. Where was the man she'd found so easy to love? Vanished, replaced by someone with a steely core. But he must always have been there, beneath the bright surface. It had taken herself to bring him out.

Fede appeared in a rush. 'Mama says you have a message for me.'

Dulcie gave it to him. He read it in a blaze of joy, and kissed the paper. Then he kissed Dulcie.

'*Grazie, grazie, carissima Dulcie.*' He glanced quickly at Guido, 'I kiss her like a brother—you don't mind—'

'Not a bit,' Guido said with a grin that would have fooled anyone but Dulcie. Now she was alive to his every nuance, and knew that his charming manners were one of the masks with which he protected himself.

'Come and eat,' Maria yelled from down the passage.

'I can't,' Dulcie protested.

'Maria will be hurt if you don't,' he said.

'But Mr Harrison wants me back—'

It was the wrong thing to say. Guido's mouth twisted in a mirthless grin.

'The man with money snaps his fingers and you go running. Yes sir, no sir, shall I break another life for you today, sir?'

'I haven't broken any lives.'

'*How would you know?*' he flashed in a voice that startled her with its bitterness, and for a moment she caught a glimpse of real pain beneath his anger. She gazed at him in the dim light, shocked to realise just how much she had hurt him. A broken life? This rich playboy who pleased himself? What could possibly touch him?

'Guido—'

She reached out her hand and in another moment she would have touched him, but then Maria yelled from the garden and he called back, 'She's just coming.'

His hand was on Dulcie's arm, gentle but insistent, and again she had the sensation of steel. He wasn't asking her, he was telling her.

The way out led to a small garden with two long tables in the centre, decorated with flowers. It was dusk, and small glasses containing candles were laid along the tables, so that on each side the faces of the Lucci clan glowed. Dulcie tried to keep up as she was introduced to Poppa, his two brothers, his three elder sons, his daughter, her husband, and various children. By that time she'd lost track.

To her embarrassment she was greeted as a heroine by everyone: Fede's friend, doing all she could to bring him together with Jenny. Since there was no way of explaining what had really happened she was forced to endure it in silence.

Fede was sitting at the end of the table. Eagerly he grasped Dulcie's hand and took her to a seat at right angles to his own. Guido seated himself facing her.

'Tell me how Jenny is,' Fede begged. 'Does she miss me? Is she as unhappy apart as I am?'

She told him as much as she could, stressing how much Jenny loved him.

'*Grazie*,' he said fervently. 'While we have friends like you and Guido I know there is still hope.'

'Be careful, Fede,' Guido said sharply. 'Have you forgotten that Dulcie came here to ruin you?'

'It wasn't like that—' she protested.

'Of course it wasn't,' Fede said at once. 'You were deluded by the Poppa, and you are our friend now, that's all that matters.' He clapped Guido on the shoulders. 'Forget it.'

'Not everyone is as generous and forgiving as you, Fede,' Dulcie said impulsively. 'Jenny's very lucky to have such an understanding man.'

'No, no, it's I who am lucky.' Suddenly he clasped her hands. 'Dulcie, you don't believe that I'm a fortune hunter, do you?'

'Of course I don't,' she said warmly, clasping his hands back and smiling into his face with as much re-assurance as she could. 'I know everything's going to work out for you, because when two people really love each other, it has to. It can't just end. It can't.'

She wondered if Guido was listening, and hearing the message she was trying to send him. Glancing up, she saw him watching her from across the table, but the glow from the candles masked his eyes.

There seemed an endless line of dishes; pasta, followed by fish, followed by veal, followed by sweet cakes. Dulcie ate heartily, which won the approval of everyone there, even Guido.

'Will you tell Jenny that I shall be waiting for her tomorrow night?' Fede begged.

'Are you going to be at the ball?' she asked.

'Not officially,' Guido said. 'But he'll be there.'

'Guido has promised to make all well, with your help,' Fede said. 'By this time tomorrow all our problems will be over.'

He bounced up out of his seat and went to help his mother at the far end.

'What mad promises have you made?' Dulcie said to Guido across the table.

He slid round into Fede's seat. 'Not mad promises at all. What I say I do, I'll do.'

'You've filled those two up with false hopes, but remember, Harlequin isn't as clever as he thinks. He'll overreach himself and fall flat on his face.'

'Not with Columbine's help. She always picks him up and remembers the things he's forgotten.'

'Don't count on Jenny.'

'I didn't mean Jenny.'

'But I'm going to be Cleopatra, didn't your shop assistant tell you?'

'Yes. A good choice. Very eye catching. Roscoe will never know that it isn't you in the costume any more.'

'And what will I be doing?'

'I'd have thought you could have worked it out by now. You slip away and change into another Columbine costume.'

'It's mad,' she breathed.

'Just mad enough to work.'

He'd put his head close to hers so that his breath whispered against her face. His eyes glinted. He wasn't reconciled to her, but her nearness affected him, as his did her. The others at the table had drawn away, smiling at these two lost in their own world.

Guido took her hand in his and looked down at it, while she felt him tremble and sensed the indecision that wracked him. Her heart ached. In a few hours she would have lost him forever unless she could find a way past the barrier he'd put up against her. And something told her that she was no nearer to her goal. He was having a moment of weakness, but he was a stronger and more stubborn man than she would ever have believed.

More of a challenge, she thought, as the gambler's instinct flared in her. But when he was gone from her life, the desolation would be the greater. She wouldn't think of that now. There was everything to play for.

Gathering all her courage she leaned forward and laid her mouth on his, feeling his shock, and his fleeting determination to resist her. Another moment and she knew that the gamble had paid off. His mind was telling him to draw back, but he couldn't do it. She'd taken him by surprise and won the first trick.

'Stop this,' he murmured against her lips.

'You stop it,' she told him. 'Tell me you don't love me.'

'I don't—'

'Liar,' she said silencing him.

After a long, intense moment she drew back a little, but not far because his hand was behind her head. His eyes, close to hers, were burning with resentment at how easily she could play on him, but still he held her face close to his. Far off she could hear applause as the family enjoyed what was happening. But the two at the end of the table weren't lovers as everyone thought. There was a deadly duel going on, with no quarter asked or given.

'Don't do this, Dulcie.'

'I will. I don't think you'll push me away in front of everyone.'

'Don't gamble on that.'

'You forget I come from gambling stock. I know more about odds than you do.'

'The odds are all in my favour. You can't win.'

'If you love me one tenth as much as you said you did, I can't lose.'

'I don't love you.'

'I say you do,' she countered.

'Is this how it has to be with you? Complete surrender? But you've already had that once. Remember that morning I came to the Vittorio and said you were my life, begged you to forgive me for concealing my identity? And all the time you knew the truth, yet you let me burble on.'

'Because I loved what you were saying,' she said passionately. 'Because I loved *you*. I remember the other things you said, too, about the years we'd spend together. It sounded wonderful.'

'Sure, it meant you'd done your job well. What satisfaction it must have given you to have me at your feet! Be satisfied with that, without trying to get me there again. Leave your victim a little dignity.'

'The hell with dignity. Look how I'm risking mine. What am I supposed to do after tomorrow night, Guido? Walk off into the sunset and spend my life in memories of a man too stupid and stubborn to see when a woman's in love with him? I told you once before, I'm not like that.'

'What are you like? How am I ever supposed to know?'

'Why don't you find out?'

'And be made a fool of again?'

The words were barely out when his lips were on hers. He wanted to quarrel with her and he wanted to make love to her, and he didn't know which one he wanted more. Then she would show him, she thought, moving in a little closer, and sensing her victory.

For a moment she thought he would fight her, but he

couldn't make himself do it. He was shaking as he slipped an arm about her shoulders, drawing her close, increasing the pressure of his mouth on hers, kissing the breath out of her. He was furious and bitter and it was all there in the way his lips moved over hers. Yet she sensed that he wasn't only angry with her, but also with himself for being unable to resist her.

Cries of appreciation went up around them but neither heard. Dulcie's heart was beating strongly, with love tinged with victory. He was still hers whether he wanted to admit it or not.

Her phone rang.

She said a very unladylike word.

Guido drew back as if shot, breathing hard and looking at her with burning eyes. Dulcie switched the phone off without answering but it was too late, the moment was gone.

'You shouldn't do that,' Guido said. 'Your employer will be angry.'

'To blazes with my employer. After tomorrow I'll enjoy never seeing him again.'

'Don't be hard on him. He did me a favour.'

Dulcie was shaking with suppressed passion and frustration at how everything had been snatched away at the last moment. Tears filled her eyes but she forced them back, determined to show no sign of weakness in front of him.

'I'd better be going,' she said.

She went round the family, saying her goodbyes and promising Fede that she would tell Jenny how much he loved her. Maria escorted her to the door, and there, to her surprise, she found Guido.

'I'll come part of the way with you,' he said.

CHAPTER ELEVEN

SHE half expected Guido to make an excuse to leave her as soon as they were out of the door, but he walked along with her for a while. He'd recovered himself now, and was on his guard.

'That was a terrible thing to say,' Dulcie said at last. 'That Roscoe did you a favour.'

'I'm sorry, I didn't mean to be rude.'

'Much I care about that!' she cried. 'That's not what this is about! We could still have it all.'

'If only that was possible!' he said at last. 'You know how much you tempt me. But it's no use.'

'Why are you so determined to hold out against me?' she asked passionately.

'Yes, I'm making a fuss about nothing, aren't I? Why should a man care if he meets his ideal and she turns out to be deceiving him for money?'

'Ideal?' she whispered, not certain that she'd heard right.

'It's a laugh, isn't it? I thought I was so street smart. Alive to every trick. Boy, was I kidding myself!'

'And that's why you hate me?'

'I don't hate you. Hating is a waste of time. It's just that you don't look the same any more, and I wish you did. The trouble with Fool's Paradise is that it's so beautiful, especially after you've been shut out. You long to find a way back in, to convince yourself that you don't know what you *do* know. Believe me, I've spent the last few days trying to get back into Paradise, even if it's only the Fool's kind. Because it's the sweetest thing that's ever happened to me, or ever will.'

'To me too,' she said wistfully. 'Is there really no way back?'

'Do you think I wouldn't have found it by now?'

'It could all have been so different, if we'd met another way.'

'The truth is,' he said wryly, 'that you have the soul of a Venetian. Tricky as they come. All the time we've known each other you've been wearing a mask.'

'Not all the time,' she urged. 'Only at the beginning.'

'All the time,' he repeated. 'When you seemed to be removing the mask you were merely changing to another. Why, you have a whole armoury of them. And who should understand that better than me?'

'I'm not the only one. You could have told me who you were from the beginning.'

'And I should have done, but I was looking at you, falling in love with you on the spot. What did names matter? I thought you were the most dazzling girl I'd ever seen and nothing else registered. Then it was too late. Besides, I get tired of my uncle matchmaking, introducing me to women who look past me to the title. You were looking at *me*, or at least I thought you were, and I couldn't resist making it last, just while we got to know each other.' He gave a crack of laughter. 'It's nauseating isn't it, like some idiot character in a fairy tale. There was me, delighted that *you* weren't a fortune hunter, and all the time you thought that *I* was.'

'You made it easy for me to think the worst. When I told you I was Lady Dulcie you went strange, as though it was important.'

'It was. I couldn't believe my luck in meeting someone that I could love and marry without my uncle giving me grief about it. I thought you were wonderful, the one honest woman in a world of schemers.' He sighed. 'Well, perhaps I should apologise for being unfair to you. It was unfair to put you on a pedestal, because if I hadn't done that I'd probably have coped better when you fell off.'

Her anger began to stir. 'Then it's as well I fell off now, because sooner or later I'd have disillusioned you. Your dreams weren't real Guido. I'm an ordinary woman struggling my way through the world as best I can. I make compromises, I don't always behave well, but mostly I just do what I have to, whether I like it or not. I'm hemmed in by circumstances, like everyone else. Except you perhaps. You've got more freedom than anyone I know. Two lives, and you hop back and forth between them to please yourself, so you can't have any sympathy with ordinary mortals.'

'You don't expect me to believe that Lord Maddox's daughter really has to do this for a living?'

'Yes, I do damned well expect you to believe it,' she flashed. 'Every penny my father had went on the "gee-gees" as he calls them, or on the tables at Monte Carlo. The estates are mortgaged up to the hilt and the bank is getting restive about the size of the overdraft. Marry me? You'd have had to be out of your mind. Dad would have touched you for a loan in the first five minutes, and if you'd been mad enough to say yes he'd have been back for more. You're better off without me. So we do agree on something. In fact I reckon I've done you a favour.'

She walked on without waiting for his reply, and he had to run to catch her up and they walked awhile in silence. Overhead the laundry hung from lines strung between buildings. Above it the moon seemed to float behind the shirts and vests. Dulcie turned aside into a dark *calle*, finding her way more readily now. He'd called her a Venetian and perhaps she was becoming one, sure-footed when faced with confusion. At any rate she moved under the single lamp, and then away from it into the gloom.

'But in the end, it's not really about money at all,' she said, her voice sounding mysterious as it whispered to him from the darkness. 'I really took this job because I wanted to punish all men for Simon. I told you about him the first evening.'

'The man you loved and thought you saw? That was real?'

'Yes, that was real. I didn't make him up. I told you we were going to come to Venice for our honeymoon, but what I didn't tell you was that it was going to be the Vittorio, the Empress Suite. He had it all planned, with me paying the bills. He thought I was an heiress. When he discovered the truth he vanished.'

Guido murmured something that sounded like a Venetian curse. 'And you came here, to that hotel?'

'Roscoe was set on it, and I thought, ''What the hell?'' What does anything matter?'

'He was here with you?' Guido asked sharply. 'In your mind, in your heart—?'

'All the way across the lagoon from the airport,' she agreed. 'All the way down the Grand Canal and right into the suite. He was there when he shouldn't have been, reminding me that he *should* have been there, and he wasn't. Always his ghost, whispering in my ear that the whole world was nothing but a great con trick, and no man was anything but a deceiver. Turning Venice into a huge, bitter joke, when it should have been so lovely—' She broke off, overwhelmed with anguish at the thought of how lovely this man had made Venice for her, how lovely he could have made the whole world.

But she had lost him, and now she was tossing her last chance away with her own hands. It was suddenly impossible to do anything else.

Guido sensed rather than saw her emotion and took an involuntary step towards her, but she backed away, fending him off. She needed all her strength to force herself to do what was best for both of them. He stood helplessly, listening to her choked breathing in the dim light.

'He was a pig,' he said at last. 'You're well rid of him.'

She gave a high, hysterical laugh. 'That's just what I thought, but here's the joke. I'll *never* be rid of him. He changed me. Men don't look the same now. I keep trying to see behind their eyes to discover what lies they're telling. When Roscoe told me what he wanted me to do I was glad. There! You want the truth, and that's it! Ugly, isn't it? Like me, deep inside.'

'I never said—'

'*I* know what I'm really like. You're only just finding out the worst. I was *glad* of the chance to hunt down and punish a man like Simon, a man who deceived a woman for her money and abandoned her when she had none.'

'And you were sure I was like this, on Roscoe's say so?'

'I saw you through the distorting lights that Simon put there. I can't get rid of those lights, and they make all men look suspicious. I guess they always will now. I am as I am. It's done. I can't change back.'

'And these were your thoughts all the time we were together,' he whispered in horror.

'No,' she whispered. 'Not all the time. When you were looking after me everything became very confused.'

'And you couldn't tell me then?'

'How could I? I thought you were Fede, and I began to think Jenny was lucky. And then I learned the truth and it was too late. I'd ruined everything, hadn't I? *Hadn't I?*'

He couldn't answer.

She was shaking with anguish as she forced the truth out. 'I've turned into someone you can't love. I guess I can't blame you for that. You loved an illusion. The real me isn't really very loveable. She's hard and cynical—'

He became angry. 'Don't say that about yourself.'

'Why not? It's what you've been saying to yourself about me these last few days. I couldn't make you happy, I see that now.' She gave a harsh, self-condemning laugh that fell painfully on his ears. 'I hated Simon so much, but it was for the wrong reasons. The real injury he did me—isn't it funny?—is to make me just like him. Do you know the saying, ''Never trust a mistrustful man—or woman''? I can't trust, and so I can't *be* trusted.'

'Dulcie,' perversely, now that she'd turned on herself, he felt the urge to defend her. But she warded him off, driven by the need to put her thoughts into words.

'We can't alter anything now, and why should we try?' she asked passionately. 'It wouldn't work. You'd never really feel you knew me, or could trust me, and how could we love each other like that?'

'You tell me,' he said, almost pleading with her. 'Columbine is the one with all the answers.'

'She doesn't know the answer to this riddle. I don't think there is one. Maybe, in the end, *I'm* better off without *you*. I'm sorry if I hurt you, Guido, but I also think you're suffering from damaged pride.'

'You really think it's my pride that's been speaking?' he asked, his voice growing angry again.

'A lot of the time. Underneath all those smiles you don't forgive easily. You believe that masks are only for you. When someone else uses them your world falls in. Pride. Well, I have pride too. It's finished. Tomorrow night belongs to Jenny and Fede, so we'll say our goodbyes now.'

'Oh, will we? Maybe I have something to say about that.'

'You've already said all I'm prepared to listen to. You win some and you lose some. I lost but there are other games to play.'

She saw his eyes gleam. 'Lining up your next victim, Dulcie?'

She was about to say that there could be nobody after him, but checked the impulse. That was weakness.

'Maybe,' she said defiantly. 'Once I've left Venice it won't matter to you what I do. But I'll say *this* before I go.'

She pulled his head down to her with a swift movement that took him by surprise. She took full advantage of that surprise, putting her arms about him, drawing his body close to hers. After a moment his arms went about her, but it was still her kiss. She was the one who took it deeper, teasing him with subtle movements against his mouth, reminding him of everything he'd thrown away.

'*Dulcie…*'

'It's over,' she murmured against his mouth. 'We might have had something wonderful but we lost our chance. I've seen myself clearly now, and I'm not the one for you.'

'Does a woman kiss a man like this when it's over?' he asked hoarsely.

'Yes, if she wants him to remember her. And I do want you to remember me.' She drew back a fraction. In the darkness Guido couldn't see her, but he could feel the whisper of her warm breath against his face.

'Remember me, Guido, but only when I'm gone. Columbine always gets away—'

'Unless Harlequin makes her stay.'

She laughed softly and it made his blood race. 'Harlequin never managed to make her do anything. He isn't clever enough.'

'That's right.' He tried to see her face, searching for something he didn't know how to find. 'Whatever he thinks, the poor sap is always dancing on the end of *her* string, isn't he?' he growled. 'Who are you? *Who are you?*'

'That's the problem, isn't it, my darling?' she asked, speaking huskily through her tears. 'You'd never really know, and it would always come between us. It's just lucky that we found out in time.'

She kissed him again, gently this time, a kiss of farewell, and slipped out of his arms. He heard her footsteps on the flagstones and at the end of the *calle* he saw her again as she reached the lights of a small canal. When she walked out of sight he waited, sure that she would return to him. But nothing happened and he began to run until he reached the canal. There was a small bridge, and on the other side he could just make out three ways she could have taken.

He tore over the bridge and stood straining his ears, hoping for some sound that would direct him. But she'd vanished into the night, and there was only the soft lapping of tiny waves against the stones. He touched his face. It was wet. But whether with her tears or his own, he couldn't have said.

Next morning the Palazzo Calvani buzzed with life like a hive of bees. Every servant in the place was on duty to make that evening's ball a success. Costumes for the family had arrived from Guido's shop and been laid out in their rooms, in readiness.

Liza was in her element, bustling everywhere, giving directions. At last she allowed herself to sit down for five minutes in the waterfront garden, and it was here that Guido found her.

'I want you to have this in thanks for what you did for me the other night,' he said. 'I should have given it to you before, but it wasn't finished until this morning.'

It was an exquisite little diamond brooch, inscribed with her name on the back. She turned it over and over, her thin face flushed with pleasure.

'*Grazie, signore*, but there was no need for any special thanks. I'm here to serve the family.'

'This was above and beyond the call of duty. Did my uncle get mad at you for losing the key?'

'He is never angry with me. Besides, I convinced him that he'd lost it himself, and he apologised to me.'

Guido's face was a study. 'I should have guessed.'

'But did it help you?'

He sighed. 'It's a long story.'

'Why don't you tell me?'

He told her as honestly as possible, not skipping his own deception, but finally coming to the point he found most painful.

'All that time, I was in love, but—I don't think she was.'

'How do you know?'

'She was pursuing me for a purpose.'

'No, she was pursuing Fede for a purpose and you confused her. And however it started, why couldn't she honestly have come to love you? You're a well-set-up young fellow, not bad looking in a poor light—'

'Thank you.'

'A bit crazy in the head, but women overlook that. In fact they sometimes prefer it. It doesn't do for a man to be too intelligent. Luckily that doesn't happen often.'

Guido's lips twitched. 'You think she might have found something tolerable in my unimpressive self?'

'Well, if, as you say, you were dancing attendance on her for days, she'd be a very strange woman if she didn't fall for that.'

He stared. 'For that?'

'Yes, that. Not your pretty face and your tom-fool jokes, or your money because she didn't know you had any, but because you were kind to her. There's something about a man's kindness that gets women in a spin. You didn't know that, did you, Signor Casanova?'

'No—I mean—of course I know that they like to be treated nicely, and I do—'

'I'm not talking about kissing their hands and buying them flowers. That's easy. I'm talking about what you did, day after day.'

'But she was vulnerable, she needed looking after.'

'The hotel would have done that, and most men would have dumped her there.'

'Leave her to strangers? No way. I wanted to know she was being cared for properly. Taking her home with me just seemed the natural thing.'

'And undressing her and putting her in your bed.'

'If you're suggesting that I—Liza, don't you dare even think—it's monstrous!'

'So you didn't?'

'No, I didn't,' he said firmly. 'I didn't even kiss her.'

'Oh, well, *that* did it.'

'Pardon?'

Liza smiled, almost to herself. 'There are times when *not* being kissed is the most romantic thing in the world. Unless, of course, you didn't want to?'

Guido groaned at the memory. 'More than I've ever wanted anything in my life. But she trusted me. Sometimes she was unconscious. On the first night she was feverish and she put her hand out and held mine, like a child. I couldn't have abused her trust.'

'According to you, she abused yours.'

'It's not the same.'

'Maybe she wasn't really unconscious at all. That was just part of the pretence.'

He shook his head. 'No,' he said quietly. 'That was real.'

'*Signore*, you don't understand being poor, like her,' Liza said firmly. 'When have you been poor as a church mouse? When it's a struggle to survive you do things you don't want to do. So she did.'

'It wasn't just that,' Guido admitted. 'There was a man who treated her badly—thought she had money and dumped her when he found otherwise.'

'*Fio di trojana!*' Liza spat.

Guido stared, for the Venetian words meant 'Son of a prostitute'. But most Venetians, himself included, would have said, '*Fio di putana,*' which meant the same, but was slightly less vulgar. Liza had expressed her contempt in no uncertain manner.

'Yes,' he agreed. 'That's what he was. It left her bitter and unhappy.' Then a burst of inspiration made him take a long breath and he said quickly, 'Her mind was clouded by misery when she first came here. She didn't mean to deceive me. She didn't really know what she was doing.'

He had it at last, the thing he'd been seeking through wretched days and sleepless nights: an explanation that would put Dulcie back on her pedestal.

'That must be it. But it's a bit late in the day to say it. My guess is that you've been hard on her. She's been judged by a man who understood nothing. And that came as a shock to her, because he'd deceived her into thinking he was kind and gentle. How could she know it was just a delusion and he wasn't really like that at all?'

'It wasn't a—OK, OK, I get the point.'

'So you thought she was perfect! Are you perfect? But like all men, you say one thing and do another.'

'When do I do that?'

'I've heard you talk about women when you thought I wasn't listening. No milksops for you, you said. You wanted a woman who'd be a challenge, you said. One who would keep you guessing, you *said*!'

There was a silence.

'I didn't exactly live up to that, did I?' he asked wryly.

'The first time you met a real woman with guts enough to play you at your own game you took fright.' Liza addressed the heavens in exasperation. 'And these are our lords and masters!'

If Guido had been less bemused he might have noticed that Liza was speaking to him with far less than her usual respect. It wouldn't have bothered him, but he would have wondered about it. Now his attention was fully occupied trying to keep up with her.

'She's too good for you,' Liza went on. 'And she was quite right to leave you. Such a pity that she'll come back.'

'You think so?' Guido asked hopefully.

'You two are fated to get married. And serve you right.'

'*What*?'

'Oh, she'll lead you a merry dance,' Liza said with relish. 'You won't know whether it's today or tomorrow.'

Guido gave her a strange look. 'I won't, will I?'

'It'll never be peaceful.'

'It'll never be dull,' he murmured.

'Whatever you expect her to do, she'll do the opposite.'

'She'll keep me guessing.'

'And you'll come by your just deserts.'

'Yes,' he breathed. 'I will.' The next moment he'd leapt up, planted a huge kiss on her cheek and headed out of the garden at a run.

'*Signore*, where are you going?'

'To get my just deserts,' he yelled over his shoulder. 'Thanks, Liza.'

He tore down to the landing stage, yelling for the boatman, who came running. Marco and Leo were in the garden. Seeing Guido speed past they exchanged puzzled glances and immediately went after him, catching up by the water.

'Where's the fire?' Marco demanded.

'No time to explain. Claudio—' this to the boatman '—the Hotel Vittorio.'

He got in and the other two joined him.

'You're not leaving our sight,' Marco said. 'You've dragged us into this stunt you're pulling tonight, and you're not vanishing, leaving us holding the baby.'

As the engine roared into life they took up position each side of him like a pair of guard dogs.

Guido slapped his back pocket. 'I've left my phone behind!'

'Use mine,' said Marco, who was never careless about these things.

Guido hurriedly dialled the hotel and was put through to the suite, but it was Jenny who answered.

'I need to speak to Dulcie urgently,' he said.

'But, Guido, she's gone.'

'Gone how? Where?'

'Left Venice. Just packed her bags and went. At least, she didn't pack all her bags because she said that stuff didn't really belong to her.'

'Didn't she leave any word for me?'

'No, she said you wouldn't want to hear anything from her.'

'The silly woman!' he yelled. 'Of course I want to hear from her. I love her.'

'Well, don't blame me. I'm not the one who's been pig-headed.'

'No, I have. But Jenny, help me put it right. What flight is she getting?'

'She's not. The flights were all booked so she's going by train. Twelve o'clock.'

'But that's only five minutes away.' He clapped Claudio on the shoulder. 'The railway station, *fast*.'

Soon the broad steps came into sight. The boat was

still a foot away when Guido leapt out. The platform for the noon train was straight ahead and he ran as though his life depended on it. He could see the train still there. Another few feet...

It began to move.

In despair he urged his legs faster and just made it onto the platform, but he couldn't catch up.

'*Dulcie*!' he roared. It was a wonder that his lungs still had any breath, but he managed to send the sound echoing down the length of the moving train.

Somewhere in the distance a head appeared through a window of one of the carriages. He couldn't see clearly but he would have known her at any distance.

'*I love you,*' he yelled. '*Don't leave me.*'

But then the head withdrew. The train was gathering speed. She was going away, and he couldn't tell if she'd heard him. Then the last carriage clattered out of sight and he was left alone on the platform, gasping and in despair.

'Let her go,' Marco advised, catching up with him and putting a hand on his shoulder.

'No way,' Guido said at once. 'I've got to get her back.'

'Phone her,' Leo said.

'Great idea.'

He called Dulcie's mobile. The train's first stop was just a few minutes away in Mestre, on the other side of the causeway. She could be back with him in half an hour.

The next moment there came the click of an answer.

'*Carissima,*' he said urgently, 'I love you. I can't live without you. I've been a pig-headed idiot but don't hold that against me. Let me spend my life making it up to you. Get off the train in Mestre, and take the next one

back to Venice. I'll be waiting right here on the platform. Just say that you forgive me and come back.
Please, *please* darling, come back. *Ti prego mia dolcis-
sima Dulcie.*'

There was a silence.

'Hello?' said Jenny's voice.

'What?' Guido whispered, in shock. 'Jenny?'

'Yes. Dulcie forgot her phone. I found it under a
cushion.'

Guido managed a polite thank you, and hung up.
'She's gone,' he groaned. 'I've lost her. There's got to
be a flight, if not from here then from Milan—'

'No!' Leo and Marco spoke as one man.

'Think of Fede and Jenny, depending on you,' Leo
pointed out.

'Besides,' Marco added practically, 'the train to
England takes twenty-four hours. You can do what you
have to at the ball tonight, catch the first flight tomorrow, and still get there ahead of her. You can even meet
her at the station.'

'That's right,' Guido said, calming down. Then he
clutched his head in despair. 'But how am I going to
get through the next few hours?'

'Because we're going to be there to make sure you
do,' Leo said firmly.

CHAPTER TWELVE

AS ALWAYS Count Calvani made sure nobody outshone him at his own ball. His long flowing robes glittered with gold thread, and on his head he wore the distinctive cap, plain at the front, raised at the rear, that said he was a Doge, one of the great men who had ruled Venice in the old days. His mask was an elaborate creation in scarlet satin, sporting tiny red and gold feathers.

He made a grand entrance into Guido's room, where his three nephews had congregated, and stood, tall and splendid, for them to admire him. When they had done so to his satisfaction he gave his opinion of their attire.

'Why are you all Harlequins?' he complained. 'The place will be crawling with Harlequins. Do you want to be mistaken for other men?'

They presented a handsome sight in their identical skin-tight costumes of coloured diamond shapes, alternating with white. Only a young man with a flat stomach and taut muscles could risk the revealing garb, and while Marco might be a fraction taller, and Leo slightly heavier, what would really distinguish them from other Harlequins was their ability to dress like this without looking ridiculous.

The costume was topped off by a small white ruff around the neck. On his head each wore a black tricorne hat, and beneath it the mask, the eyebrows raised to give a quizzical look. Francesco snorted.

'I suppose you're planning something disgraceful, like making inroads among the female guests and leaving them wondering which one of you it was.' He then spoiled his righteous indignation by adding, 'That's what we did in my day.'

'I don't think our chaste ears are ready to hear about your youth, Uncle,' Leo said, grinning.

'You'd get a few surprises,' Francesco agreed. 'But now I'm a reformed character. Guido, you'll be glad to hear that I'm going to do what you've always wanted.'

'Get married?' Guido gasped.

Marco coughed. 'But Uncle, isn't it a little late for you to be thinking—I mean—'

'I'm in my prime,' the count declared firmly.

'Of course he is,' Guido said. 'The nursery will be full in no time.' An agreeable vista of freedom was opening before him. 'Will we meet her tonight, Uncle?'

'No, she won't be at the ball.'

'But surely—?'

'Any more than Lady Dulcie will be at the ball,' Francesco said, glaring at him. By now he knew that they'd met, but Guido hadn't burdened him with too many precise details. 'I won't ask what you've done to offend her, but I'm sure it's something unforgivable.'

'She seems to think so,' Guido grunted. 'I aim to put it right soon, but now that my marriage will no longer matter to the family line, since you're marrying yourself, I'd rather discuss it no further.'

When Guido spoke in that firm tone nobody argued with him. A few minutes later they were all on their way downstairs to meet the torchlit procession that was coming along the Grand Canal. Gondola after gondola approached the landing stage to be greeted by their hosts, and a stream of masked figures passed into the glittering palazzo.

Music was already playing. Lights shone from every

door and window. A line of footmen stood bearing trays on which stood glasses of the finest crystal, filled with the best champagne.

'If only they'd show a little originality,' Francesco growled as he stood waiting, a smile fixed on his face. 'So many Columbines, Pantelones, Pulcinellas.'

'They can't all be the Doge of Venice,' Guido muttered. 'Not many men could carry it off.'

'That's true,' Francesco agreed, mollified.

'And if you want something unusual,' Leo said, 'how about Henry VIII?'

The Vittorio motor launch was just drawing up, with Roscoe standing in the rear.

'Roscoe Harrison,' Guido said. 'You are delighted to see him.'

'Am I?'

'For my sake, yes. The Columbine in the back is his daughter Jenny.'

'Another Columbine! How many is that?'

Guido need not have feared. The count gloried in his skills as a host, and the next few minutes went smoothly. Francesco bowed low over Jenny's hand murmuring, 'How charming!' and he and Roscoe eyed each other's attire with respect.

Guido took charge of the new arrivals, feeling Jenny cling nervously to his arm, and led them into the house. He would have been glad to skip this evening which was going to be so different from his hopes. Dulcie should have been around, helping him out, and then, while they were working together—here his invention failed, but surely something would have happened. He scowled. When Harlequin ran out of ideas Columbine was supposed to come to his rescue.

He'd managed to get a seat on an early flight next

morning. In the meantime he had work to do. He studied Jenny, noting with approval that she'd dressed to his instructions, with a black silk cap concealing her hair, a small black tricorne hat and a crimson satin mask, so heavily trimmed with lace that it covered most of the lower part of her face as well.

Her dress was a mass of white tulle, with a tight waist, puff sleeves and a huge ballerina skirt that ended just below the knee. She looked delicate and enchanting.

'Fede won't be able to resist you,' he said when he'd swept her away into the dance.

'Oh, Guido, is he really here? I'm so nervous.'

'He's outside in the boathouse. We'll wait until it's a bit more crowded and your Poppa can't see you so well, and then my brother Leo will ask you to dance. Your father will think it's me, but I'll be dancing with another Columbine and so we'll keep him confused.' His gaze fell on a detail that troubled him. 'I wish you weren't wearing that diamond necklace. It looks like it cost a fortune.'

'Ten thousand,' she said with a sigh. 'Dad insisted on giving it to me just before we came out. He said it was to "console me" for losing Fede.'

'That figures. But you can bet he'll keep his eyes on it, and it'll complicate the switch over to the other Columbine. I've persuaded one of the maids to help out.'

'It was supposed to be Dulcie, wasn't it? She's really gone then?'

'Yes, but I'm going to get her back. Jenny, I simply must talk to you about her.'

'We will, I promise. But I see Dad waving to me. I'll be back later.'

She slipped away and Guido lost her in the crowd. He spent the next half hour on hot coals, doing duty dances, watching the time pass, wondering how soon he could get away to England.

Roscoe was enjoying himself. He and the count had squared up to each other, and he hadn't backed down. And those diamonds of Jenny's! Anyone could see that they'd cost a pretty penny. It never hurt to show people you had money, and Roscoe had big plans for his daughter.

He looked around and frowned when he couldn't see her. She'd been there just a moment ago, dancing with Guido. Then she'd vanished in the crush.

No, there she was again, a pretty Columbine, threading her way through the crowd, her diamonds sparkling magnificently.

'They look wonderful on you, darling,' he growled.

But Columbine didn't seem happy. She made a gesture as if to remove the diamonds, but he stopped her.

'You keep them on. Guido was looking at them. Keep working on him, and you'll be a countess yet.'

Columbine sighed and began to thread her way back through the crowd to where Harlequin was looking around him.

'There you are,' he said with relief.

'You wanted to talk about Dulcie.'

'I'm going to follow her to England.'

Columbine put her head on one side, teasing him. 'And when you see her, what will you say?'

He groaned. 'I don't know. Just ask her to forgive me for being a pompous jerk, I suppose. Who knows what she's thinking now? I don't even know if she heard me calling to her down the platform. She didn't telephone you?'

'I haven't spoken to Dulcie,' Columbine said truthfully. 'And even if I had, I doubt she'd tell me much. Once she's made up her mind, that's it!'

Through his mask Guido's eyes widened with alarm. 'You don't mean that she'd never forgive me? I don't believe that.'

'Dulcie's stubborn. When she's decided against somebody—' she gave an eloquent shrug.

'But you don't really know her well.'

'Neither do you after just a few days—'

'A few days is enough when you've met your ideal. Or a few minutes. I knew at once, when she tossed that sandal down into my gondola—'

'But you didn't know she threw it,' Columbine reminded him. 'You thought it was fate but actually it was her. I think she was dreadful, deceiving you like that.'

'But she didn't deceive me,' Guido said earnestly. 'Not if you look at it the right way. Dulcie and I were always destined to be together, so when she threw that sandal she was only doing what fate demanded. And when I let her think I was Fede, that was fate too, because that way she saw *me*. Not a Calvani with a palace and a title at his back, but just a man falling in love with her.'

He wondered if Columbine would speak, but she danced in his arms, gazing intently at him, as if she were waiting for something. He was several inches taller, and from this angle he could see little of her lower face, because the lace of the mask blocked his vision. But he could see her green eyes, and a strange feeling began to creep over him.

'I'll make her listen to me,' he said. 'I'll remind her what it was like during those days we spent together, because that's when we were most truly ourselves. She was so—' he hunted for the word, not easy for him, a man not used to analysing '—so surprised. As though nobody had ever taken care of her before.'

'That's very clever of you,' Columbine said thoughtfully. 'I don't think anyone ever really has. The rest of her family were so irresponsible that she couldn't afford to be. She had to grow up too fast and she's been lonely all her life, but people don't see it.'

'I once told her that masks could make people free to be their real selves,' Guido said. 'Now I think maybe your real self can come as a surprise. I'm not who I thought I was.'

'Who are you, Guido?' Columbine asked earnestly. 'Do you know now? And do you know who she is?'

'I'm the man who loves her, come what may,' he said.

'But is she the woman who loves you? Suppose she doesn't?'

'She must, even if I have to spend the rest of my life convincing her.'

Columbine smiled as though she'd discovered a secret treasure. But instead of answering him directly she said, 'Someone's trying to attract your attention.'

Guido saw two Harlequin figures beckoning him from the window that led into the garden. He murmured something to Columbine and followed to where Leo and Marco were waiting for him.

'It all went like clockwork,' Leo said from behind his mask. 'We delivered Jenny to the church, Fede was waiting for her with his family, and they're probably married by now.'

'But Jenny's still here,' Guido said thoughtfully. The

strange, haunted feeling was back. 'I was just dancing with her.'

'Jenny was with us.'

'Then who—?' He remembered now. Jenny's eyes were blue.

Dazed, he returned to the ballroom, looking this way and that, searching for Columbine. But, like an elusive ghost, she'd vanished.

Suddenly there seemed to be a thousand Columbines, and none of them was the right one.

What he was thinking couldn't be true, he told himself. It was a mental aberration. But while his head might be muddled his heart had never been more clear. He knew everything now. Or at least, Harlequin knew what Columbine thought it was good for him to know.

He spotted her at last, drinking champagne and talking to Leo, who'd removed his mask. Suddenly inspired, he made sure his own mask was in place, and bore down on them.

'You'd better keep out of Guido's way,' he said, clapping his brother on the shoulder. 'That little revelation has put him on the warpath.'

'So I saw,' Leo said, studying him cautiously. 'Marco?'

'Sure, I'm Marco, and I'm about to ask this lady to dance.' He slipped his arm firmly around Columbine's waist, and glided with her onto the floor. Her eyes were on his face, laughing, not fooled one little bit.

'So Guido's annoyed?' she asked provocatively. 'Serve him right!'

'Don't be so hard on him,' Guido said. 'He's not a bad fellow.'

'He's a clown and someone should take him in hand and reform him.'

'You can do that when you're married.'

'Me? Marry him?' Columbine sounded shocked. 'Never!'

'You've got to marry him,' Harlequin said urgently. 'You can't leave him running amok the way he is. Think of the family reputation. Besides, he's madly in love with you. I know he hasn't been clever about it, but you can be clever for both of you. After all, you're really in love with him too, aren't you? Otherwise you wouldn't abuse him so much.'

'Never mind about Guido,' Columbine said, looking at her partner's mouth and thinking how badly she wanted to kiss it. 'After all, he isn't very interesting.'

'You don't think so?'

'I've never thought so,' she said with a fair assumption of indifference. 'But I played along to keep him happy.'

Their eyes met through the slits in their masks, each understanding the other perfectly.

'You—' he breathed, 'you—I've a good mind to—'

'To do what?' she asked with interest.

'To do *this*!'

Swiftly he removed his mask, then hers, and pulled her into his arms for a long, breathless kiss, while the crowd cheered and applauded.

'It was you all the time,' he said when he could speak.

'I fooled you for a while, didn't I?' Dulcie teased.

'Only a very short while,' he growled, interrupting himself with another kiss. 'How did you get here?' he asked breathlessly after a while. 'You were leaving.'

'I left the train at Mestre and caught the next one back. Not just because you came after me. I was going to do it anyway. I stormed off because I was furious, but I wouldn't really have let Jenny and Fede down.'

'I see. You only came back for them?'

She chuckled. 'Of course not. There was another reason.'

He held her tightly. 'Tell me.'

'I had to retrieve my mobile phone,' she teased.

'*Cara*, you'll drive me too far—' he broke off. She was laughing at him and it was like music.

'I would always have come back,' she said, 'because I wasn't going to give up on us just like that.'

He kissed her again and again, while the music played and they swayed in its rhythm.

'So,' she resumed as he whirled her about the floor, 'at Mestre I telephoned Jenny, and she told me about your calls, and the very interesting things you'd said.'

'But why not call me?' he demanded. 'You knew I loved you. I should think the whole world knew after I shouted it the length of the platform.'

'I did call you, but Marco answered. You'd all just got back from chasing me to the station. Leo was there too, and they told me one or two things—'

'Like that I was going out of my mind. Just tell me how big a fool you've all made of me.'

'I came back, Leo met me at the station and brought me here. Then I just slipped into the role you'd always meant me to play, wearing the costume you supplied. Roscoe complicated things by giving Jenny that necklace, but in a way it actually made things easier. Jenny gave it to me just before she left, and while I wore it nobody doubted that I was her.'

'And you made the switch—when? When Jenny saw Roscoe waving to her. She left me—'

'Slipped into a side room, where Leo and Marco were

waiting, gave me the necklace, and told me you wanted
to speak to her about me. They left. I went out to speak
to Roscoe—'

'And he didn't know his own daughter?'

'He knew his diamonds, which were all he was looking at. I came back to you and took up the cue she'd
given me, about you wanting to talk about Dulcie.'

'But why couldn't you simply have told me?'

She chuckled, and the sound went through him pleas-
urably. 'I wouldn't have missed the last hour for anything. I've discovered things I couldn't have learned any
other way.'

'And of course you've enjoyed setting me up.'

She tilted her head. 'That's Columbine's nature, I'm
afraid. Harlequin will just have to learn to cope with
her.'

'Will she always be with him?'

'Always in his hair,' she assured him.

'Always in his life, in his heart?'

'Wherever he wants me.'

He kissed her again. When she opened her eyes they
were dancing past Roscoe, whose eyes were popping at
the sight of her. It would soon be time for explanations,
but just now she wanted to talk to nobody but Guido.

'When did you know?' she asked.

'It was your green eyes. Jenny's are blue. And then
Marco and Leo told me Jenny had left, so I couldn't
have been dancing with her.'

'Did the plan work?'

'Like a dream apparently. They took her to a little
church where a priest was waiting. By the time Roscoe
sees them again they'll be married. And talking of marriage, I have a confession. I can't make you a countess.

Uncle Francesco is going to get married and have a son, to cut me out. He's promised.'

'Don't be silly! As though I cared about being a countess.'

'Then there's nothing standing in the way of our marriage.'

'I didn't say—'

'You have to marry me, after all those things you said to Marco.'

'I haven't spoken to Marco since the ball started.'

'You started this dance with him.'

'Yes, but that was you.' She eyed him with suspicion. 'And what am I supposed to have said?'

'You said you couldn't live without me, and you'd die if I didn't propose.'

'In your dreams!' she said wrathfully.

'But you already fill my dreams, *carissima*, and you always will. What's a poor fool to do?'

She couldn't help laughing at his serpentine way with the facts. She was dealing with a master of deception. But not all deceptions were bad.

'Don't worry,' he said. 'I'm quite prepared to marry you to save you from going into a decline. *Don't do that!* I'm ticklish!'

'That'll teach you to get funny with me,' she murmured into his ear, so that the soft whisper of her breath sent him into a whirl.

'Darling,' he said ecstatically, 'am I going to be a hen-pecked husband?'

'Definitely.'

'You'll teach me how to say, "Yes, dear", "No, dear"?'

'Can't start too soon. And if you're out late I'll be waiting for you with a rolling pin.'

'I *adore* you!'

'I hate to break up the happy dream,' Marco said, appearing beside them, 'but Signor Harrison is getting agitated.'

He and Leo stationed themselves protectively as Roscoe approached. Dulcie removed the diamond necklace and handed it to him.

'I promised Jenny I'd see this safely returned,' she said. 'She didn't feel she could accept it since she was doing something that you wouldn't like.'

'And just what does that mean? Where the devil is she?'

'Signora Lucci is just leaving for her honeymoon with Fede,' Guido announced. 'The bride and groom are very happy.'

Roscoe's eyes narrowed. 'What are you talking about? Where's my Jenny? If she thinks she can defy me—'

'She's already done it,' Dulcie said. 'She's married the man she loves. Please Roscoe, try to be happy for her.'

'Happy? You did this. I trusted you, and I ran up bills to keep you here. Well, you can pay for all those posh clothes *Lady* Dulcie, and see how you like that!'

Guido stepped forward. 'As Dulcie's future husband let me say that I'll be glad to refund you every penny you spent on her clothes—and then dump the lot in the lagoon. And if you dare speak to her like that again, you'll follow them. Do I make myself plain?'

Roscoe squared up to him, but there was something about Guido at the moment that made his courage fail. He took a step back, covering his retreat with sharp fire.

'I'm done with the lot of you. And you can tell that

precious pair that they'll never get a penny of my money. Not a penny.'

'Good,' Guido said. 'Stick to that. They'll be a lot happier.'

Roscoe gaped. He just didn't understand.

'He won't stick to it,' Dulcie said when Roscoe had stormed off. 'Like she said, he doesn't have anyone else.'

'*My boy*!'

Francesco bore down on them in grandeur. He kissed Dulcie, wrung Guido's hand and flung his arms out as if to say that he'd brought the whole thing about.

After that there were toasts and then more toasts, and the ball went on into the early hours. A light was already appearing on the water as the gondola procession wended its way back, and the family was left alone. Francesco embraced Dulcie again.

'I knew as soon as I met you that you were the only woman who could keep him in order,' he declared.

'And what about you, Uncle?' Leo demanded with a grin. 'Guido says you're making plans too. One wedding begets another.'

The count raised his hand for silence.

'This is true. I have finally managed to persuade the only woman I have ever truly loved to become my wife.'

While his nephews looked at each other in bafflement he went to the door, opened it, and reached out to somebody outside. In a gentler voice than they had ever heard him use, he said, 'Come, my darling.'

There was a tension-filled pause, then Count Calvani's future bride appeared, and everybody stared with astonishment.

'*Liza*!' Guido gasped.

'I have loved her for years,' Francesco said simply.
'Many times I've begged her to marry me, but she always refused. She said I would be marrying beneath me, which is nonsense, for she is the greatest lady in the world.'

Liza smiled at him, and for a moment they could all see her as Francesco did, as the sweet-faced girl who'd come to work there nearly fifty years ago, and won the young count's heart on the first day. She was arthritic, elderly, and she was the greatest lady in the world. For a moment Dulcie's eyes misted over.

Guido was the first to embrace Liza and call her 'Aunt'. Marco and Leo followed.

'There's no escape for you after all,' Marco told Guido with a touch of malicious relish. 'You'll have to put up with being the count.'

'Get lost,' Guido growled.

'Do you mind very much?' Dulcie asked gently.

'Are you still going to marry me?'

'Of course I am.'

'Then I don't mind anything else.' He took her hand possessively, drawing her away from the others and leading her out to the peace of the garden.

There they faced each other with truth between them at last.

'No masks now,' she whispered.

'No, masks, *carissima*. Never again. Not between us.'

He took her face between his hands, searching it, as if for the first time; seeing there everything he wanted in life, wondering how he could ever have been so blind.

'Say my name,' he begged. 'Mine, not Fede's.'

'Guido,' she said softly.

In response he spoke her own name, over and over, making it music.

'How could I have misunderstood you?' he asked. 'I knew from the start that there was only truth and honour in you. The rest was an illusion.'

'Darling, it wasn't,' she began to protest.

'Yes it was,' he said quickly. 'I saw it clearly today. You were so unhappy that you weren't yourself. It coloured everything you did, as though someone else was doing it. Now the real you has come back, the woman I couldn't help loving.'

'You're saying dangerous things,' she said, swiftly laying her fingertips across his mouth. 'I can't live on a pedestal. I'm human. I'll disappoint you and fall off.'

'Ah, but you can't,' he said eagerly. 'Because I'm going to make sure you're never, ever unhappy again. So that solves the problem, don't you see? It's easy.'

She made one last effort. 'Don't think me better than I am.'

'I shall think of you what I please,' he said, smiling and stubborn.

He was incorrigible, she thought. And he always would be.

She had told him that she was as she was, but the same was true of him. It was buried deep in his nature, this need, not merely to love but to idolise. He'd tried being angry with her, and hated the feeling so much that in future, if disillusion threatened, he would tap-dance his way around awkward facts, so that his precious image of her would remain undisturbed. And so, throughout all their years together, she would be incapable of doing wrong in his eyes.

It was wonderful, but it was an awesome responsibility. For a moment she almost quailed under it, but his eyes were upon her, full of warmth and passionate adoration. He'd laid a heavy burden of trust on her, but his love would always be there to bear her up.

He drew her close and kissed her. It was nothing like the tormenting kisses they'd given each other last night, after the dinner with the Luccis: nor the exuberant embrace of the ballroom. This one was quiet and full of many promises. One journey had brought them safely home into each other's arms. Another journey was about to begin.

'Now you're mine,' he said quietly. 'And I shall never, never let you go.'

Three months later there were two weddings at St Mark's Basilica. It wasn't a double wedding because Liza dreaded being the centre of a large crowd and Francesco, after loving her so long, would do anything she wanted.

So they married quietly in a small chapel, with only the Calvani family present, and as soon as the wedding was over the new countess insisted on busying herself with the final preparations for the second wedding next day, to which most of Italian and English society had been invited.

At the reception and dance afterwards the two bridal couples took the floor, amid applause. And there was another couple, drawing curious eyes as they danced in each other's arms.

'Marco and his fiancée seem very happy,' Guido observed as they paused for champagne.

'You sound surprised,' Dulcie said. 'I thought you liked Harriet when we went to their party in Rome a few weeks ago.'

'I did. I do. It's just that there's something about that engagement that I don't understand.'

'Well, it certainly came about very suddenly,' Dulcie agreed. 'Harriet just appeared out of nowhere, and suddenly they were engaged.'

'Are they in love, do you think?'

Dulcie regarded Marco and his fiancée, Harriet d'Estino, gliding gracefully by. 'I don't know,' she said thoughtfully. 'But you've got to admit that what happened at that engagement party was very strange.'

'Strangest thing I ever saw,' Leo observed over her shoulder. 'Marco was a lot more upset than he allowed to appear. You know how he keeps his feelings to himself. And he wouldn't tell the world he was in love, either.'

'More fool Marco,' Guido said, his loving eyes on his bride.

The wedding was a lavish extravaganza, which neither of them had wanted, but also which neither of them noticed. Today they were the centre of a performance, wearing the glamorous masks that the world expected, playing their parts to perfection. Tonight all masks would fall away, and so now they could be patient, waiting for their moment.

Nobody knew the honeymoon destination. Several were mentioned—New York, the Bahamas, the south of France—but never confirmed. Only Liza knew that when, late in the evening, they slipped away from the reception, they headed, not to the airport, but to the landing stage where a gondola awaited, with a familiar gondolier keeping it safe.

'Fede!' Guido shook his friend's hand warmly, and Dulcie kissed him.

'Here it is,' Fede said, indicating his gondola. 'Jenny

asked me to say sorry she left the reception early. She was feeling a bit queasy, and Roscoe got rather over-protective.'

'How is the future grandfather?' Dulcie asked.

'Trying to take over, but we're resisting. He's almost as hard-going now as when he was hostile, but Jenny's happy, and that's all that matters.'

He helped to settle Dulcie in the boat, handed the oar to Guido, and retreated, waving.

Dulcie sat facing Guido, her bridal veil billowing around her. 'Let's go home,' she said. 'Our real home.'

He began to ply the oar. 'You're sure you want to have our honeymoon there? We could still fly away if you like. Anywhere in the world.'

'But we have the world waiting for us,' she said softly.

He headed out into the Grand Canal, then turned the gondola into the small canals for the short journey home.

The palace and its turmoil slid away from them. The glitter faded into the distance. Music floated faintly across the water. Under the stars Harlequin and Columbine drifted in an endless dream.

Dare to Dream...

Every woman has dreams—long-cherished hopes, deep desires, or perhaps just little everyday wishes!

In this brand-new miniseries from

Harlequin Romance®

we're delighted to present a series of fresh, lively and compelling stories by some of our most popular authors—all exploring the truth about what women *really* want.

May: THE BRIDESMAID'S REWARD by Liz Fielding (#3749)
June: SURRENDER TO A PLAYBOY by Renee Roszel (#3752)
July: WITH THIS BABY... by Caroline Anderson (#3756)
August: THE BILLIONAIRE BID by Leigh Michaels (#3759)

Look out for many more emotionally exhilarating stories by your favorite Harlequin Romance® authors, coming soon!

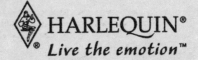

HARLEQUIN®
Live the emotion™

Visit us at www.eHarlequin.com

HRWWWA3

If you enjoyed what you just read,
then we've got an offer you can't resist!

Take 2 bestselling love stories FREE!

Plus get a FREE surprise gift!

Clip this page and mail it to Harlequin Reader Service®

IN U.S.A.
3010 Walden Ave.
P.O. Box 1867
Buffalo, N.Y. 14240-1867

IN CANADA
P.O. Box 609
Fort Erie, Ontario
L2A 5X3

YES! Please send me 2 free Harlequin Romance® novels and my free surprise gift. After receiving them, if I don't wish to receive anymore, I can return the shipping statement marked cancel. If I don't cancel, I will receive 6 brand-new novels every month, before they're available in stores! In the U.S.A., bill me at the bargain price of $3.34 plus 25¢ shipping & handling per book and applicable sales tax, if any*. In Canada, bill me at the bargain price of $3.80 plus 25¢ shipping & handling per book and applicable taxes**. That's the complete price and a savings of 10% off the cover prices—what a great deal! I understand that accepting the 2 free books and gift places me under no obligation ever to buy any books. I can always return a shipment and cancel at any time. Even if I never buy another book from Harlequin, the 2 free books and gift are mine to keep forever.

186 HDN DNTX
386 HDN DNTY

Name	(PLEASE PRINT)	
Address	Apt.#	
City	State/Prov.	Zip/Postal Code

* Terms and prices subject to change without notice. Sales tax applicable in N.Y.
** Canadian residents will be charged applicable provincial taxes and GST.
All orders subject to approval. Offer limited to one per household and not valid to current Harlequin Romance® subscribers.
® are registered trademarks of Harlequin Enterprises Limited.

HROM02   ©2001 Harlequin Enterprises Limited

eHARLEQUIN.com

Becoming an eHarlequin.com member is easy,
fun and **FREE!** Join today to enjoy great benefits:

- **Super savings** on all our books, including
  members-only discounts and offers!

- Enjoy **exclusive online reads**—FREE!

- Info, tips and **expert advice** on writing
  your own romance novel.

- FREE romance **newsletters,**
  customized by you!

- Find out the latest on your
  favorite authors.

- Enter to win exciting **contests
  and promotions!**

- Chat with other members in our
  community message boards!

**Plus, we'll send you 2 FREE Internet-exclusive
eHarlequin.com books (no strings!)
just to say thanks for joining us online.**

——— To become a member, ———
visit www.eHarlequin.com today!

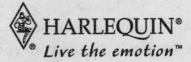